WAITING
FOR THE
RAIN

A RICHARD JACKSON BOOK

WAITING
FOR THE
RAIN

A novel of South Africa

SHEILA GORDON

Orchard Books · New York and London

A DIVISION OF FRANKLIN WATTS, INC.

ORCHARD BOOKS
387 Park Avenue South
New York, New York 10016

ORCHARD BOOKS OF CANADA
20 Torbay Road
Markham, Ontario 23P1G6

Divisions of Franklin Watts, Inc.

MANUFACTURED IN THE UNITED STATES OF AMERICA
Book design by Tere LoPrete

10 9 8 7 6 5 4 3

The text of this book is set in 11 pt. Waverley.

Library of Congress Cataloging-in-Publication Data
Gordon, Sheila.
  Waiting for the rain.

  Summary: Chronicles nine years in the lives of two
South African youths—one black, one white—as their
friendship ends in a violent confrontation between
student and soldier.
   [1. South Africa—Race relations—Fiction. 2. Race
relations—Fiction. 3. Friendship—Fiction] I. Title.
PZ7.G65937Wai 1987   [Fic]   87-7638
ISBN 0-531-05726-7
ISBN 0-531-08326-8 (lib. ed.)

WAITING
FOR THE
RAIN

PART ONE

CHAPTER

1

*T*he second thing Frikkie always did when he arrived at his uncle's farm for the school holidays was look for Tengo. But first, he would run around exploring his favorite places to make sure that nothing had changed.

He would go first to the barn where the bales of hay were stacked, yellow and sweet-smelling, to the roof. Then he would race across the yard to the cowshed and greet the cows by name, patting his favorites on their warm glossy haunches and stroking them between their calm, mild eyes as their tails twitched away at the flies buzzing in from the glaring sunshine outside. Sarie . . . Marie . . . Tessie—creamy white, highly pedigreed, and dignified—who yielded the most milk of the herd. His uncle, Oom Koos, had gone overseas, to Scotland, to buy Tessie. "Cost me a fortune but worth every penny," he always said as the buckets frothed up with her rich creamy milk under the supple black fingers of Timothy, Tengo's father, who was the boss-boy on the farm.

When he had greeted all the cows and smelled their

warm sweet grassy breath, Frikkie would cut across the stretch of veld beyond the fence to see how the ears of corn were ripening in the acres of cultivated fields that stretched away to the horizon. He would examine an ear of corn as he had seen his uncle do, separating the silky tassel to peel back a leaf of husk and dig his thumbnail into the milky white kernel. Then he would run down the hill behind the farmhouse and throw himself onto the grassy riverbank, where the willows dipped their fronds in the water running clear over the flat, round stones. Schools of tiny fish darted about in the shallows, and the deep water gave back the reflection of the hard, bright blue of the Highveld sky with massed white clouds sailing across it. Through the branches of the willows the sun dropped flecks of light that lay like gold pennies under the water.

The grass was alive with busy insect life, and the cicadas chirped their cheerful, unchanging song in the sunshine.

When he had made sure that everything was just the way he recalled it during the grinding boredom of the school term, Frikkie would stand up, brush the grass from his clothes, and go to look for Tengo.

Frikkie's uncle—Oom Koos he was called in Afrikaans —and his aunt, Tant Sannie, had no children of their own. Frikkie spent all of his school holidays on the farm. He lived in a small town about a hundred and fifty miles away, with his mother and father and sister. His father was a municipal clerk; his mother taught typing in a business school; his sister was called Henrietta, but everyone called her Sissie, just as his name—Frederiek—had become Frikkie. One of his teachers at school who came from England complained about the way South Africans gave their children proper names and then always called them by nicknames instead.

Ever since Frikkie had first been brought to visit the farm when he was no more than a baby, he had loved this place better than his parents' house in the town. He didn't care for school. He liked being busy, felt cramped and restless at the scarred inky wooden desk in a classroom smelling of chalk and pencils and the lunches packed in the pupils' schoolbags. Even while he was out on the sportsfield playing soccer or cricket, he would have preferred to be helping Oom Koos on the farm.

As the end of the school term came near, he would take out a ruler and pencil and a sheet of squared paper, fill the paper with neat blocks, and pin it up on the wall of his room. Every night, when his homework was done, he would fill in one of the blocks with a crayon.

"What are you doing?" Sissie asked him.

"When all the squares are filled in," he explained, "it will be time for me to go to the farm." He looked at the drawing Sissie was making with colored crayons. "What's that supposed to be?"

"Can't you see! It's Oom Koos's farm."

"Why do you use those colors? The veld is green and the sky and river are blue."

"Ach, the veld is brown and yellow and dry and dusty and boring, and lonely. And the insects bite. And there's nothing to do there and no one to play with except the kaffir children. It's better to stay here in town for the holidays."

"I love the farm," Frikkie told her. "Even in winter when everything's dry and brown. I wish I didn't have to go to school. I'd rather be at the farm than anywhere else in the world."

"Don't you miss Ma and Pa? At night? When you're in bed? It's so quiet there. I get scared."

"That's what I like—the quiet. Better than the noise of the traffic up and down the road. I'm never scared there. I'm as used to Oom Koos and Tant Sannie as I am to Ma and Pa."

"I *hate* the farm." Sissie screwed up her face and banged her fist on the table.

"I hate coming back to school at the end of the holidays. Oom Koos is teaching me to be a real farmer. He says when I finish school I can come and work for him and be the farm manager."

"Won't you *ever* come home?"

"Oh, I'll come and visit you and Ma and Pa sometimes. When you're grown up and married, you can bring your children to stay there. Oom Koos says if I turn out to be a good farmer, he'll leave me the farm when he dies."

"Is he going to *die?*" Sissie asked, her eyes and mouth open wide.

"Not for ages and ages, *domkop*," Frikkie said. "I'll be a pretty old guy myself by then." He took up a green crayon, and Sissie watched as he carefully filled in a blank square until not a trace of white showed.

Frikkie looked for Tengo in the garden to see if he was weeding Tant Sannie's flowerbeds or vegetable patch. He wasn't there, nor was he in the dairy or in the fields where the harvesting of the *mielies* had begun. He went back to the house and into the kitchen where Selina, Tengo's mother, worked as the cook and housemaid.

"Selina!" he called out.

Selina came out of the cool stone pantry with a basin of potatoes.

"Hau! *Kleinbaas* Frikkie!" she said, calling him "little master." His uncle was called *oubaas*, "old master." "When did you get here? Tengo will be glad to see you."

"I came all by myself—in the train," he told her, pleased with himself. He had turned ten that year, and it was the first time he had been allowed to travel alone. "I even had to change trains at Boesmanskloof. My uncle picked me up at the station."

"You are getting to be a big boy." Selina sat down heavily at the big scrubbed deal table and started peeling potatoes. "Tengo is four months older than you. I think you are already taller than he is."

"Where is he, Selina? I've been all over the farm looking for him."

"Oh, I sent him down to the kraal with the milk for my mother. His little sister, Tandi, she is not well. She won't take any food, except milk, and she's crying all the time."

"My mother sent Tandi some of my sister's clothes that she's grown out of, Selina. I'll bring them to you when I've unpacked."

"It is kind of your mother, kleinbaas," Selina said. She sighed, dropped a peeled potato into a dish of water, started on another.

"I'm going to find Tengo." Frikkie went out through the screen door of the kitchen into the sunshine, past the chickens clucking and scratching in the fowl run, through a gate and down a dusty dirt road that led over the veld to the kraal—a group of round mud huts with thatched roofs where the farmworkers lived. Sissie's brown and yellow crayons were the right colors here. Here the ground was hard, flat, parched, with scrubby clumps of grass and black, jagged thornbushes covered sparsely with leaves. Way ahead, beside a stand of bluegum trees, smoke rose from the cooking fires in the kraal. Behind him, in the hot, still afternoon, a rooster crowed in the farmyard.

He came to a gate, unlatched it, and went through, closing it securely behind him. As a small boy he had once left this gate open when he had gone down to the kraal to play with Tengo. The cows had got out and gone crashing through the growing corn, and Oom Koos and the boys had had a hard time rounding them up. That was the first and last time Frikkie had ever left a farm gate open.

Now the road sloped down a low rise, and in the valley Frikkie could see the circle of red mud huts with their straw roofs like neat, shady sun hats. The sound of a dog barking drifted over the quiet, sweet-smelling air; it was one of the thin, scraggy yellow farm dogs that hung about, half wild, near the kraal, and it barked monotonously as if it knew no one would take any notice. It was a lonely sound. Frikkie wished someone would throw it a scrap to quiet it.

CHAPTER

2

*T*engo was sitting on an upturned box playing with a lump of red clay. Inside the hut his little sister cried, and his grandmother's voice crooned soothingly. Behind the hut a straggling vegetable garden grew—a few pumpkins ripening among large prickly leaves, potatoes, carrots, rows of beans. His mother and father were busy from early morning until dark working for the oubaas, and there was never enough time to tend the garden. Tengo did some weeding when he could, but fetching water from the dam was hot, heavy work; and the earth swallowed up the water so thirstily that by the time he was back with the second pailful, the place he had watered looked dry already.

Beyond the garden a yellow mongrel dog kept barking and barking, but there would be no scraps to throw it until tonight when they had had their evening meal. From the top of the hill where the farmhouse stood, he heard the rooster crow.

His grandmother came out of the hut. She looked worried. "Why are you sitting here just playing, Tengo?" she said. "Aren't you supposed to be up there collecting the eggs?"

"I already have given the eggs to the madam. My father said I don't have to go back until milking time. Look what I've made, Granny." He held up a small cow he had modeled out of clay. It stood in the palm of his hand—rounded haunches, slender legs, its face mild, its tail to one side as though it had just switched at the flies.

"Hau!" his granny said. "It's just like a real, living cow." She shook her head in wonderment.

"Tengo! Tengo! Where are you?" a voice came calling out over the veld.

"The kleinbaas has come." His grandmother shaded her eyes with her hand and looked out past the bluegum trees.

Tengo placed the clay cow carefully on the ground and stood up as Frikkie came into the circle of huts.

"Tengo! I've been looking everywhere for you. I came on the train. All by myself. I had to change at Boesmanskloof. Hullo, Lettie," he greeted the old lady.

"Hullo, kleinbaas. You're getting big, hey?"

"What's this for?" Frikkie picked up a lump of clay. "What are you making, Tengo?"

Tengo pointed to the cow.

Frikkie squatted down to take a look at it. "You made that!" he said. "Who showed you how to do it?"

"No one. I just made it."

"Let's see it." Frikkie put out his hand to take it.

"*Don't touch it!*" Tengo shouted.

Frikkie looked up at him, startled.

"It's still soft," Tengo explained. "It has to dry out in the sun."

"Who gave you the clay?"

"I dig it up next to the *dam* where the cows drink."

"I'll race you to the gate," Frikkie said.

The two boys ran off together. The old lady sat down on the box and watched them. Her eyes were not so strong any more, and she could not make out which one of them reached the gate first. In the hut the child was quiet now. She hoped the sickness was not a bad one. Her daughter Selina had already lost two children through sickness, and Tengo and Tandi were all she had now to take care of her when she grew old.

The dog had run off at Frikkie's approach, but it was back again, barking, barking, as if it expected nothing.

Without discussing it, Tengo and Frikkie made straight for the small valley where the river ran, the sun beating down on them as they crossed the shadowless veld. "Last one in's a monkey!" Frikkie shouted as they pulled off their shirts and waded into the water in their shorts. Frikkie had had swimming lessons at school, and a few summers ago he had taught Tengo to swim. The water was not very deep, but it was cool and pleasant, and they splashed about, ducking each other and throwing water in each other's faces. Then they lay on the grass, the sun's heat so strong that they could feel their clothes drying on them.

"I wonder how it feels to swim in the sea," Tengo said.

"My friend at school told me it makes your mouth taste of salt, and the waves are so strong they knock you over."

"Did he tell you what the sea looks like?"

"It's like a very, very big dam, Tengo, that reaches so far that it touches the sky. And on the other side of it there's another country."

"I'd like to see the sea," Tengo said.

As they crossed the farmyard, Tant Sannie came to the kitchen door. "Frikkie, come inside. It's teatime. Your uncle's already at the table. Wash your hands and go and sit down."

"Wait for me, Tengo," Frikkie said. "I won't be long. I want to show you the new cricket bat I got for my birthday."

It was cool in the dining room, with dark, heavy old furniture that had belonged to Frikkie's great-grandparents who had bought the farm when they had just married. Their framed pictures hung on the wall. They looked very old-fashioned to Frikkie—she in a poke bonnet and a dark dress with a lace collar; he with a long dark beard and a hat with a high, round crown. A strip of flypaper hung from the light fixture, a newly caught fly buzzing angrily as it tried to free itself from the sticky surface already dotted with dead insects.

Oom Koos was stirring his tea, the teaspoon small in his thick-fingered, sunburned hand. Tant Sannie poured the tea from a big brown teapot, added milk and sugar, and passed it to Frikkie. She cut him a slab of her homemade fruitcake.

Frikkie took a bite of the cake, sweet and rich with fruit, farm butter, and eggs from their own hens. "This is the best cake in the world," he said, and drank some hot, strong tea. "And this is the best place in the world."

His aunt and uncle laughed.

"I wish I never had to go back to town."

"Listen to the child," his aunt said fondly. "And this is only his first day here."

"You do your work well at school," his uncle told him, "and when you're a big fellow and you've passed your matriculation exams, you'll come and work here and stay here—for good."

Tant Sannie put another slice of cake on his plate.

When tea was over, Selina cleared the table. In the kitchen, she poured the tea that remained in the pot into a large, chipped enamel mug, stirred in sugar and milk. She put the cake away in a tin in the pantry, cut a thick slice of white bread which she spread with apricot jam, then took the bread and tea out to Tengo who was bouncing a ball in the yard.

In a moment Frikkie came out with a cricket bat and ball. Tengo was sitting on a wooden bench in the shade of the jacaranda tree, having his tea; Selina was taking sheets down from the wash line. Frikkie liked the fresh, sweet smell of laundry that had dried in the sun. At night, when he got into bed in his room at the farm, his sheets and pillowcases gave off the scent of sun and clean country air.

"Hurry up with your tea, Tengo. I want you to bowl for me." But Tengo took his time, enjoying the soft, white, jammy bread and the sweet, strong tea. Around him the blue-mauve jacaranda blossoms drifted down, forming what looked like a blue lake in the middle of the yard. It was a huge, old, thick-limbed tree, planted by Frikkie's great-grandfather.

Frikkie squatted down and fitted tubular jacaranda blossoms like glove fingers onto his hands. He wiggled them in front of Tengo's face. "I am the monster and I will gobble you up if you don't quickly finish your tea and come and play cricket with me," he roared.

Tengo emptied the mug and plate and left them on the back doorstep; he turned and caught the hard, heavy cricket ball that Frikkie threw.

"Don't play near the house," Tant Sannie called out. "I don't want any windows smashed, thank you."

Tengo bowled and Frikkie batted, swiping at the ball with his new bat, sending the ball over the veld for Tengo to retrieve. Tengo went on bowling until he saw his father driving the cows across the fields toward the barn. He ran across the yard to open the gate.

"I was just going to give you a turn to bat," Frikkie called out, following him.

"I have to go and help with the milking now," Tengo answered.

In the milking room each cow, udders swollen with milk, knew its place at its own stall and started to feed at the fresh mounds of hay while the farmhands settled beside them on low stools, shoulders pressed against the cows' flanks. Soon the sound of contented munching blended with the hiss and spurt of the milk hitting the insides of the metal pails.

Frikkie felt himself filled with happiness. These were the sounds, the smells, the tasks he dreamed about as he sat over his books in his desk at school. He stood beside Tengo, watching the black fingers working the creamy white teats as if they were playing a musical instrument. The milk spurted rhythmically, foaming up as the bucket filled. "Let me have a go, Tengo," he asked.

He took Tengo's place on the stool.

"Hold it—so," Tengo instructed him. "Press your fingers against your thumb—stroke—*stroke—don't pull!*" he shouted as the cow shifted uneasily. It switched its tail, flicking Frikkie's nose; and as he jerked backward a stream of milk squirted up, hitting them both full in the face. Both boys fell about laughing, Frikkie wiping the milk from his face and hands with his shirt.

"Look out, you two," Timothy reprimanded them. "If

the oubaas comes in and sees you getting up to nonsense, there'll be trouble."

"But I want to learn how to milk," Frikkie protested.

"You get on with it then, Tengo," his father told him.
"Kleinbaas Frikkie, you come and sit here by me, and
I'll show you. Like so . . . like so . . . squeeze and stroke—
not too hard, not too soft. Strip it down . . . strong and
easy . . . strong and easy . . . otherwise you get nothing
but an empty bucket."

By the time Frikkie had filled a quarter of the pail his
fingers were aching and he gave up.

"Come and practice a little bit every day, kleinbaas,"
Timothy told him as he took over. "Then you will learn
to milk as good as Tengo."

Frikkie went back to watch as Tengo emptied the
udder; it hung soft and slack now, and the cow looked
contented. From a hook Tengo took down a metal mug,
dipped it into the frothing pail, and handed it to Frikkie.
Frikkie drank. It was still so warm it felt heated, sweet,
thick with cream. He put his head back and drained the
last drop.

"You've got a white mustache," Tengo teased him.

He wiped the froth from his lips with the back of his
hand. Now Tengo took the cup, dipped it, and drank.

"Now *you've* got a white mustache," Frikkie said.

"If the oubaas catches us drinking raw milk we'll get
in trouble," Tengo told him.

"Then wipe your mustache away and hang up the
cup, and no one will know."

Outside, the sky had reddened as the sun sank in a
fiery ball onto the horizon. The crooked thorn trees stood
out black against the glow. Some low cloud had turned
purple, rimmed with orange radiance, the veld rolling
away in gray-blue billows till it met the sky. The milk-

ing done, the milk cans filled and lined up in the dairy, Tengo and his father set off with the other workers for the kraal.

"See you tomorrow, Tengo," Frikkie called out. He walked back across the yard. Dusk was gathering around the farm buildings, creeping in under the jacaranda tree, the fallen blossoms black now that the color had drained from the sky. Across the yard drifted the smell of meat stewing with vegetables. Oblongs of yellow light fell from the house across the dark ground. Through the window he could see Selina in her blue overall with a flowered kerchief tied around her head, stirring a pot on the stove.

The good smell of food made Frikkie feel hungry. He hurried indoors into the brightly lit kitchen.

CHAPTER

3

*W*hen Frikkie went back to town at the end of the holidays, Tengo felt bored and lonely, restless. Frikkie always complained about having to go back to school, but Tengo wanted to know about many things that puzzled him, and he knew that if he could go to school he would be able to find out about them. He wanted to know why the sea was salt and the water in the river was sweet; why the clay he dug at the dam was good for modeling animals and figures, but the clay from the riverbank crumbled when it dried; why the thunder always rumbled after the flash of lightning and not the other way around; why mosquitos bit you, and butterflies didn't. He wanted to know about the country that lay on the other side of the sea—what the people there were like, whether they also ate meat with their porridge, how they talked. Questions came all day into his mind, and there was no way of answering them.

He didn't think he would ever get to see the sea. It was hundreds of miles away his father had told him, and train tickets were expensive. But he knew that a book was like a magic thing—it was small enough to hold in your hand and yet you could take from inside it something big like the sea and the waves and high mountains; and you could find inside it how people live in that country on the other side of the sea, what they eat, what they say to each other, what kind of houses they live in.

There was no school for the farm children to go to. The nearest school was in a village fifty miles away. Tengo's mother had gone to a school run by missionaries when she was a child, and she had taught Tengo to read and write and add and subtract and do the multiplication tables. But he had no way of getting books to read; there was barely enough money for his parents to get food and clothes for the family. He had read the few tattered schoolbooks they had, over and over, until by now he knew them almost by heart. They were too easy for him.

His mother worried about him. She wanted him to be educated, but since two of her children had died—one of them while she was staying with relatives so that she could attend the village school—she was afraid to let Tengo out of her care. The relatives lived on the outskirts of the village in a native reservation for the members of their tribe. Tengo's grandfather had been one of the elders of the tribe. But he was dead, and the tribe was poor, and an extra mouth to feed would be a burden on them. And there was no money to spare to pay for the child's upkeep if they sent him to school there.

Tengo was very quick to learn. The oubaas had already said that if he remained on the farm one day he would become boss-boy. The oubaas was quite kind. He didn't pay them much, but he gave them bags of cornmeal and plenty of milk, so they never were really

hungry. They ate meat rarely, but they grew their own
vegetables. And at Christmas the oubaas would slaughter
a cow for all the workers in the kraal, and there would be
great feasting and everyone's belly would be full for a
change.

If ever one of the older farm children left to go to
school in the village, Tengo's mother would notice that
for a few days Tengo went about very quiet and re-
served, and her heart would feel sore as she watched him.
"When you are a little older, Tengo," she would promise,
"when you're bigger and stronger, we'll let you go away
to school."

Tengo watched his grandmother as she cooked the evening meal. He thought about Frikkie on the train that
was taking him back to school. Another thing Tengo
couldn't understand and would have liked to look up in
a book, was why everything was free at Frikkie's school,
while the parents of the black children in the reservation
had to pay for schooling and books. Tengo had never
been on a train. Sometimes, waking late at night, he
could hear the distant roar of the freight train passing
through Doringkraal, the hoot of the train whistle float-
ing over the dark veld, and he would long to be rushing
through the night on a train taking him to a place he
had never seen.

In the three-legged black iron pot that simmered over
the fire, bubbles exploded as the steam broke through to
the surface of the thick white cornmeal porridge. His
grandmother stirred the pot with a big wooden spoon
and hummed a little crooning chant in a low voice. On
the ground beside her was a basin of creamy curds of
milk. They never drank the milk fresh. It was their

custom to let it sour in the sun and then spoon up the tart curds.

Over on the other side of the kraal the boys were kicking a soccer ball about; some girls were laughing and plaiting one another's hair. Tandi, his little sister, was playing outside their hut. She was better now, but their mother worried because she was thin and listless. She was playing with a little clay family Tengo had made for her. There were a mother and father and two children, all made of red clay, and a small round hut with a roof of real thatch. He had even made some tiny pots of clay, and Tandi was pretending to cook dinner for her toy family, stirring a three-legged pot with a small stick.

"Frikkie has gone back to school," Tengo said to his grandmother. "He didn't want to go. He says school is boring. But I think it's boring not to be able to read and learn."

His granny sighed. "You should ask him to bring you back some of his old schoolbooks. Then you could study from them."

Ezekiel, the oldest man in the kraal, came by and stopped to chat with them. He was tall and thin and wiry but stooped now with age. He was an elder of the tribe and had been boss-boy on the farm for the father of the oubaas. Now he was too old to work, and the oubaas gave him a small pension of ten rand a month, and allowed him to stay on at the kraal. He sometimes did light jobs at the farmhouse.

One by one Tandi handed Ezekiel her clay toys for him to admire. He held them close to his eyes, peering at them and chuckling. "Hau, Tengo," he said. "The spirit of one of your ancestors is in you." He sat down on an upturned box. "I remember—when I was a small boy, the age of Tandi—there was this old, old man, your grandfather's uncle. He would carve figures out of wood, and they were full of life, just as yours are."

"Did he make toys?" Tandi asked.

"No, my child. The figures he made were used for magic ceremonies. They contain secrets. If there was drought, he would make the figure that would bring rain. If there was a quarrel with another tribe, he made masks for the men to wear when they danced the dance asking the gods to secure us the land where we grazed our cattle."

"He was my relative?" Tengo asked, pleased that the old woodcarver's spirit helped him when he modeled. His figures also contained secrets. . . .

"Yes," the old man said. His eyes looked out over the twilit veld as if he could see things that had happened long, long ago.

An old person's memories are also like a book, Tengo thought; they are filled with stories of the time that our time comes out of.

"And he told me," the old man went on, "that *his* grandfather also had the skill of carving wood."

"Frikkie told me that his family has been in this district going back many grandfathers."

The old man chuckled. "My child, long, long before the kleinbaas's grandfathers came here—long before any white man came here at all—our tribe was here. This was always our land—the land of our tribe."

Here was another puzzle now that Tengo would have liked to find the answer to in a book.

"It's true what he is saying," his grandmother agreed, stirring her pot. "Our dead are buried here for many generations. We have been here long before the white man came." The gate on the farm road slammed shut. "Here is your father," she said. She shook up the dented black iron pan in which vegetables were stewing on her stove made out of an old square paraffin tin perforated with holes. Through the holes red-hot coals glowed.

Tengo's father chatted for a while with Ezekiel, who then went off to his own hut where his granddaughter-in-law was preparing his food. Tengo and his family settled down to their meal, eating seated around the fire, scooping mounds of the porridge from the pot with their fingers and dipping them in the savory stewed vegetables. His mother ate dinner with the family only on Sundays, her day off. Since she had to cook dinner every night up at the farm for the oubaas and his wife, she could not get back to the kraal in time. She would cook her own pot of maize-meal porridge—and after she had served dinner and washed the dishes, she would eat it at the kitchen table with whatever was left over from their meal.

Tengo's father took an envelope from his pocket. "Here is a letter from your auntie in Johannesburg. She's asking if your cousin Joseph can come and stay here for a few weeks. He has been sick, and they think he will get better here in the country and the fresh air. I asked the oubaas, and he says it will be all right—if he doesn't stay too long."

Tengo felt very happy when he heard this. He hadn't seen his cousin for a few years. Joseph was four years older than he and clever and funny. He lived in a black township outside Johannesburg, a big city with buildings so tall, Joseph had told him, that people went up and down in them in electric boxes; and whole families lived one above another, until the building almost reached the sky.

"When will he come?" Tengo asked his father, full of excitement.

"I will answer the letter tonight, and the oubaas will post it tomorrow when he goes to Doringkraal. Then they will send a telegram telling us which day he will arrive."

After their meal Tengo watched his father sharpen a pencil with his penknife and settle down with a lined notebook on his lap to write the letter by the light of a candle. Beyond the leaping shadows, at the back of the hut, his sister and his grandmother were asleep in the bed they shared. He so looked forward now to his cousin's visit that he no longer minded so much that Frikkie had gone.

Tengo and Joseph sat in the shade of the willows beside the little river. Since there were no places in the big city where black people could swim, Joseph had never learned how, and Tengo had been giving him lessons. By the second week Joseph could stay afloat quite well, but Tengo said he was splashing too much and had to try to improve his stroke. They were cool when they came out of the water; but the sun was so strong that the water quickly evaporated off their skin, and soon they felt hot again.

Joseph was not as funny and lively as Tengo had remembered him. He had grown tall; he was thin after his illness, quieter, as if his mind was elsewhere. He was fourteen and in the seventh grade at his school in the township.

It was very still in the heat of the afternoon. Nothing moved; only the cicadas whirred cheerfully in the tall grass.

"You're lucky you live in the big city, Joseph," Tengo remarked.

"Lucky?"

"Sure. You go to school and learn about everything. I'm always asking myself questions, and I have no way of finding the answers."

"You're lucky to live on the farm, Tengo. Believe me. It's quiet here. And clean. And it smells good. In the township, man, Tengo, there's always a terrible smell. Smoke and petrol fumes and dirty toilets and garbage—garbage everywhere. . . . And the houses are so close to each other, you hear people talking, fighting, babies crying, crying. . . . Noise—noise the whole day and the whole night. And there are *tsotsis*. . . ."

"Tsotsis?"

"Bad people. Kids. They don't go to school—maybe their parents haven't got money for school fees or books. Or they play truant; their parents are away all day working in the city. The kids steal and fight and smoke and drink and mug people. Everybody's scared of them. They're tough, and they show off, and they carry knives."

Tengo's eyes were wide. "Don't the police catch them?"

"Oh yes"—Joseph gave a little laugh—"they catch them all right. And they put them in jail. And in jail they're with such *bad* people—real criminals—that when they get out they're even worse than before—really wild. And they don't care any more. Man, you really have to watch out for the tsotsis. And you have to watch out for the police as well."

"The police? Why?"

"Passbooks."

"Passbooks?"

"Tengo, it's true, you really don't know very much." Joseph laughed and shook his head and gave Tengo a friendly punch on the arm. "Man, you know that all

black people have to carry a pass. *You'll* have to have
one when you turn sixteen, with your name and birthday and address and where you work and where you
come from—your whole life history. Your father has one,
but on the farms no one asks to see it. But in *town* it's
your permit that lets you live there and work there. You
have to carry it with you *always*, and you have to show
it to a policeman any time he asks to see it." Joseph
grabbed Tengo by the shoulders and shook him roughly,
talking in Afrikaans like a policeman: "Pass, kaffir—
where's your pass? Where's your pass, kaffir?" Then he
let go of Tengo and laughed.

Tengo looked astonished. "But what if you don't have
your pass on you—if you left it at home by mistake?"

"Jail. They take you straight to jail." Joseph dangled
a willow branch into the water, and a school of small
fish, in one movement, changed direction and moved
on. "I wonder if one fish is the leader and the others
just follow him," he said.

But Tengo was not thinking about the fish. "Joseph,
do you mean that even if you haven't done anything
wrong they can put you in jail?"

"They say you've done something wrong if you don't
have your passbook with you *all the time.*"

"Can't you tell them you'll go home and fetch it?"

Joseph shook his head.

"So if your father is coming home from work and he
hasn't got it with him, they can take him away to jail?"
he asked.

"That's right. It has happened to my father," Joseph
said bitterly. "To my friends' fathers. You pay a fine or
stay in jail. And if your book isn't stamped with a permit
that says you are allowed to be living where you are,
you have to leave the city and go back to your kraal."

"Hau . . ." Tengo shook his head. "I wouldn't want to live in the city, Joseph." He felt lucky, now, that his father worked for the oubaas, not even a mile away from the kraal, and came home every night across the veld and through the farm gate without any policeman trying to stop him.

Joseph slid into the river, scooped up handfuls of water and threw them over Tengo. "Man, Tengo, you really are a *domkop*," he said. "You don't know *anything* about apartheid."

"Apartheid?" Tengo went and sat on a large flat stone and dangled his feet in a pool. "What's apartheid?"

"It's the law of the white man that keeps them masters, and us servants." He splashed Tengo again, teasing him. "Where's your pass, kaffir? Where's your pass?" Then Joseph pulled Tengo into the water and ducked him.

For the remainder of his stay Joseph didn't want to talk about his life in the city. If Tengo questioned him, he would say, "Forget about it, cousin." He would suggest instead that they go and swim or help with the milking or kick the soccer ball around on the hard, red, dusty earth of the courtyard surrounded by the huts of the kraal. When the ball sometimes landed among the scrawny hens busy pecking away near the bluegum trees, they would squawk angrily, fluttering their wings and scuttling away under the trees. The boys would shout with laughter.

"Don't frighten the chickens," their grandmother reprimanded them. "If they are upset, they won't lay eggs."

When Joseph went back after two weeks on the farm, he looked better and was more cheerful. Selina gave him a letter to her sister, his mother, who worked in Johannes-

burg, asking her if she could manage to send some books
for Tengo to read and study from. She wrote the letter
at the kitchen table in the farmhouse while her madam
was taking her afternoon nap.

The child is very anxious to learn. We don't have
the money for books, and neither do you, I know.
But I remember that the people you work for have
children, and perhaps they will give you some of
their old schoolbooks for Tengo. . . .

The oubaas took Joseph to Doringkraal in the pickup
truck when he was going in to buy fertilizer. His wife
told Selina to make some sandwiches for Joseph for the
journey, and the oubaas gave him a handful of small
change from his pocket when he dropped him off at the
station.

When Selina came back to the kraal that evening after
her day's work at the farmhouse was done, she found
Tengo sitting glum beside the brazier of glowing coals.
He was watching the gray layer of powdery ash forming
as the red-hot coals cooled.

"Missing your cousin already?" she asked.

He nodded.

"I'm sorry, my child." She sat down on the upturned
box beside him and patted his head. She didn't want to
mention the letter she had written, in case it would raise
his hopes and the books did not come. "It isn't so long
now before the Easter holidays, and the kleinbaas will
be back and you'll have someone to play with. Oh, I'm
tired. . . . She stretched her arms and looked up at the
vast black sky thick with stars. "Look, quick, Tengo—
there—a shooting star!"

They watched as the brilliant ball with a long tail of

glittering silver dust trailing behind it fell across the dark night to disappear as silently and mysteriously as it had come.

"That means good luck," his mother said. She thought, Maybe it means my sister's madam will send books for the child. "Oh," she groaned, "I am so tired tonight. The madam and I have been making fig jam today. It's hot work stirring, stirring that big iron pot over the fire all day. Whew!" She opened her cracked plastic shopping bag. "Here's a bottle of jam madam said I could take for us."

But Tengo wasn't thinking about fig jam. He was wondering what a shooting star was, where it came from, why it fell through the sky just then, where it went when it could no longer be seen. And during the day, he wondered, when the sunlight made it too bright to be able to see the stars, were shooting stars falling through the sky just the same?

CHAPTER

4

*I*t was Saturday when Joseph arrived back in Johannesburg. On the outskirts of the city the train passed by the mine dumps, high, flat hills of yellowish sand that had piled up in the early years when gold had first been discovered here. Deep mine shafts and a network of tunnels had been carved out underground to reach the rock in which the ore was locked. Stripped of their gold now, sometimes in the abandoned hollowed-out caverns beneath the ground there would be great rumbling falls of rock, and earth tremors would shake the city, startling people awake in the middle of the night and causing high buildings to sway and small objects to fall off shelves. Bare and ugly, with nothing growing near them, the mine dumps guarded the approach to the city, and on windy days the hard dry grit blew off them and settled in layers of pale dust on windowsills and furniture in the houses of the town.

Joseph was to take the bus from the station to the house in the suburbs where his mother worked as the cook. The next day was her Sunday off, and they would return together to the township. There was a long wait for his bus. Several red-and-white double-decker buses came lumbering by, but they were for white people only. At last it came along, a rattling green single-decker, and Joseph rode through the center city, past shops and high office buildings. Soon there were apartment blocks, parks, trees, shopping centers, then green suburbs with fine houses set in beautiful gardens. From the bus window Joseph glimpsed over walls and hedges the blue-green glint of swimming pools in many of the gardens. He saw the flash of water as people splashed about in the bright sunshine of the summer afternoon, and figures of sunbathers on long chairs and on clipped smooth lawns.

The shopping center near where his mother worked was bustling with Saturday afternoon shoppers. Joseph studied the faces in the crowds, hoping, as he always did, that among them he would see his father; he would jump off the bus and run, pushing past the crush of people until he reached him. . . . They had not heard from his father in a long while. He had worked for many years for a small dry-cleaning company, but the owners, fearing that trouble was coming to this country, had closed their business and gone to live overseas. His father's permit to live in the city was good only as long as he had a job; without a permit he was unable to look for work. He had been arrested a couple of times and then had become afraid to go out of the house in the township where he lived with his wife's relatives. And one day he had left. For a while letters had come from the Transkei, where his grandfather worked a small plot of land. But now the letters had stopped. His mother wrote, but there was no answer. One of these days, she said, she would like to go to the Transkei to look for him. But meanwhile

she had to keep working to support them. She could not
go away.

Joseph pulled the bell cord and got off the bus. He
walked through the quiet green suburb. Only black
people were on the streets—servants who worked in the
big houses. The whites went everywhere in their cars.
Black nursemaids pushed prams with white babies in
them. He came to a house with a pair of high ironwork
gates. On a gatepost was a well-polished brass plate with
a name: Dr. David Miller. Here Joseph's mother, Matilda, had been working for many years, even before he
was born. When he was a baby, she used to work with
him tied to her back in a blanket, but once he began to
walk she had had to send him to live in the township
with her brother and his wife and four children and
mother-in-law.

Joseph went through the gate and up the driveway. On
the tennis court one of Dr. Miller's daughters was having
a game with three friends. She waved to him as he
passed by on his way to the back yard. There were five
children in the Miller family, and their mother was
always taking and fetching them to and from school and
dancing classes and music lessons and tennis lessons and
extra coaching at exam time. Joseph's mother told him
that the madam never sat down for five minutes. The
gardener was watering the flowerbeds and turned the
spray off to have a chat with Joseph. At a table under a
tree in the yard, Dora, the housemaid, was polishing
silver knives and forks and spoons. "Hau, Joseph!" she
called out. "Your mother has been looking out the door
for you since lunchtime. Here you are at last."

The kitchen door was open, and his mother was inside
baking a cake. She was very pleased to see him, to see
how much better he was looking after his stay in the

country. He sat down at the kitchen table, and she gave him a mug of tea and a plate of sandwiches. "Your appetite is back," she said as he bit hungrily into the bread. "I can see you are cured now, my boy."

While he ate, she mixed the cake batter with an electric mixer, scraped it into a cake tin, and set it in the oven to bake. The Millers were kind people to work for. They always helped the servants with money or time off when they were in trouble. They had paid the bail money when Joseph's father had been arrested, but there was nothing they could do to fix up his job permit. "It's lucky for us that the master's a doctor," Matilda always told new servants when they came to work here. "He looks after us when we're sick, and he gives us free medicine." It was the master who had told her that Joseph needed a holiday in the country after his sickness, and he had given her the money for his train ticket.

Joseph was to spend Saturday night with his mother in her room in the servants' quarters at the far end of the yard, though it was illegal for anyone other than registered servants to sleep there. The master wanted to give him a checkup to make sure he was quite well.

While the cake was baking, Joseph told her about his holiday. Then she settled at the table to read the letter he had brought from her sister on the farm. Joseph looked at some comic books one of the Miller children had left on the countertop. The kitchen filled with the good smell of butter and sugar and vanilla as the cake began to brown. The telephone rang and Matilda answered it.

"Dr. Miller's residence. No. The doctor is playing golf this afternoon." She wrote down a message from one of his patients, then finished reading the letter.

Outside, a car door slammed, and the madam came in from the garage through the kitchen door. "Joseph! You're back. Any messages, Matilda?"

"On the message pad, Madam."

She put a paper bag of shopping on the counter. "Put all this in the fridge before it melts, Matilda. I'm so hot I'm going right in for a swim." She read the messages on the pad. "Why won't they give the master some peace at the weekend," she complained. "There'll only be ten for dinner, not twelve, Matilda. My cousins aren't coming. That cake smells delicious. Have you made a fruit salad?"

"Yes, Madam."

In the doorway, she paused. "Joseph looks much better, don't you think, Matilda?"

"Yes, Madam. He had a good holiday on the farm."

"Has he had something to eat? The child needs to put on some weight."

"He's eaten, thank you, Madam. Madam, my sister has sent me this letter with Joseph. Her little boy, Tengo —Joseph's cousin—he's a very clever child. But he doesn't go to school. My sister's afraid to let him go away from home because already two of her children have died. But he wants very badly to learn, Madam, and there are no books for him to study with. So she's writing to ask if Madam would send some of the children's old school-books for him to study."

"How old is he, Matilda? Ten? The house is over-flowing with the children's old books. Write down the address for me. We'll make up a parcel and send them."

"Thank you very much, Madam. Your cousin Tengo will be pleased, eh, Joseph?"

Joseph nodded.

"Don't leave before the master gets back, Joseph," Madam said. "He wants to examine you to make sure you're quite well now."

"He's staying here overnight, Madam," Matilda told her. "Tomorrow's my off, and we'll go back to the township together."

"Oh, are *you* off tomorrow. I thought Dora was. Make sure there's something cold for lunch then, Matilda. My brother and his family are coming for the day."

"Yes, Madam. And Madam, Joseph wants to say thank you to you and the master for paying for his train ticket."

Joseph stared at the cover of a comic book, remaining silent.

"Oh, as long as it did him good . . ." the madam said. "It's so *hot* in here with the oven on, my dress is sticking to me. I must go in for a swim. Matilda, be a dear and bring me a tray of tea at the pool." She went out.

Matilda folded the letter and put it in her apron pocket. She filled the teakettle and put it on to boil. "Well, Tengo will get books now," she said. "When Madam says she will do something, she does it."

Joseph stared at the cover of the comic book and said nothing.

CHAPTER

5

Oom Koos drove into Doringkraal every weekday to pick up the mail, farm supplies, provisions from the general store. One morning, after he had collected a heavy spare part for his tractor at the station depot and picked up a spool of brown thread for Tant Sannie at the draper shop, he stopped off at the post office for his mail.

The postmistress asked him to come around behind the counter to collect a large cardboard carton that was too heavy for her to lift.

"It's not my birthday," he joked with her. "Who's sending me presents?"

"It's not for you, *Meneer*," she said. "It's for one of your kaffirs at the farm."

When he got back to the farm, he saw Timothy carrying fresh hay across the yard to the milking stalls. "Timothy," he said, "there's a parcel for Tengo from Johannesburg. A heavy cardboard box marked *books*. What can a piccanin do with a box of books if he can't read?"

"He can read, Master. But now he wants to learn. To study."

The farmer laughed. "Tell him if he gets too clever he won't be able to stay on the farm. It's a heavy box. I left it in the back of the truck."

"Thank you, Master."

Timothy always took his midday meal at the farmhouse. When the sun was directly overhead in the hard blue sky, and the shadows shrank under the trees like dried-up pools, he splashed his face and arms at the pump in the yard and sat down at the table under the jacaranda tree where some small shade collected. Selina came out of the kitchen with his tea and bread and jam. On the bench beside him was the large cardboard carton.

"What's that?" she asked.

He smiled. "It's from Johannesburg. It must be the books for Tengo."

"They've come!" she said. She clapped her hands with pleasure. "Thank God! Matilda's madam is a good woman. Have you told Tengo?"

"He doesn't know yet. He's out with the cows."

"Oh, he's going to be so happy," she said. She went back inside to prepare lunch for the oubaas and the madam, lugging the package with her. She set it down on the floor in a corner of the kitchen. She hummed a cheerful tune as she set the table, stirred the soup, sliced the cold mutton very thin, and arranged lettuce leaves around it. Each time the carton caught her eye, pleasure warmed her heart.

When Tengo came to the kitchen door to get his bread and tea, he said, "My father told me there is a surprise for me."

"Come inside." His mother's cheeks plumped up with her broad smile. She showed him the carton.

"What is it?"

"Books."

"Books? For me? Where from?"

His mother put her arm around him and squeezed his shoulder. "Books—for *you*. Your auntie's madam in Johannesburg has sent them. Should we open it now?"

Tengo stared at the cardboard carton as if it were a magic object. "No. I'll open it tonight. At home."

Tengo had once played with a helium-filled balloon that Frikkie had brought to the farm. He had liked the way it tugged at the string, filled with lightness and wanting to take off, to float away. For the rest of the afternoon, as he went about his tasks on the farm, he felt as if his heart was like that balloon. Each time he thought of the box of books, saw it in his mind on the floor of the farm kitchen, he felt his heart tugging inside his chest, full of lightness, wanting to float off up into the pure high blue of the sky.

After work that evening Timothy walked home across the veld, strong and upright with the box of books balanced on his head, while Tengo scampered happy and excited beside him.

He could not ever remember being so happy as each book was taken out, examined, and marveled at. The hut, in the warm flickering glow of the candlelight, seemed to him to be an enchanted place.

The Millers had sent an assortment of old schoolbooks —history, geography, nature study—all of them filled with pictures and maps and drawings. His grandmother and father and Tandi exclaimed as each book was taken from the box, and they leafed through the pages admiring the illustrations. There was a paperback dictionary, and none of them could work out what it was until his mother came in from work and explained how it was used. And there were story books. His mother sat down on a chair with her plastic shopping bag still looped over her arm and started at once to read them a story about a girl called Goldilocks who gets lost and finds herself in a house belonging to three bears.

"*Bears*?" Tandi asked. "What are *bears*?" And Tengo pointed to a colored picture on the opposite page and said, "Here, silly, can't you see? *These* are bears." And their old grandmother kept saying "Hau . . ." and shaking her head in wonderment.

Tengo wanted to start right in and read all of the books at once. Deciding which one to begin with filled him with the pleasure he felt when he held a piece of pliable, worked clay in his hand and wondered what figure—what small person or animal—was hidden inside the clay, waiting for him to set it free. . . .

His mother arranged the books on a shelf, and had Tengo start off with the easiest. She showed him how to use the dictionary. The more he read, the better he became at it. He spent less time modeling clay animals now. While he was out herding the cows, or milking, or mopping down the floor of the dairy, he would think about the wonders of the world the books were opening out for him. And from the story books he began to gain some idea of what that land was like on the other side of the sea.

One afternoon, as he came to the last page of *A History Reader for Primary Schools*, he closed the book and looked out over the veld, and he remembered something that had happened the previous year that he had not

liked to think about because it made him feel unhappy.
Sissie had come with Frikkie to spend the short Easter
holidays at the farm. He and Frikkie had come into the
kitchen from the fowl run with the eggs. His mother
was at the sink scouring a pan; the madam was rolling
dough at the kitchen table, and Sissie was sitting beside
her reading out loud from a story book. Her elbow was
on the table, her cheek resting against her palm, and in
a high clear voice she read without stopping or stumbling or needing to use her finger to guide her along—as
if reading were the easiest thing in the world.

His mother had called him and he had gone into the
scullery, but he hadn't heard what she was saying to
him. All he could hear was that high piping voice
effortlessly reading words that he would have been able
only to struggle with, words he would have had to sound
out, using his finger as a pointer and waiting for the
letters to take shape and meaning in his mind. She was
three years younger than he, and she could read more
easily than he could. It had made him feel very bad, as
if he had tasted something bitter.

And the taste would not leave him. When he and
Frikkie went outside to play, he kept missing the ball
and not listening to what Frikkie was saying, hearing
only Sissie's high, babyish voice reading the words so
easily. . . .

Now the reading was coming so easily to him that he
was sure he could read words that would be too hard
for that silly little Sissie.

Now he always took a book up to the farm with him
in the morning, and whenever there was time to spare
he would find some shade and settle down to read. If the
oubaas wanted him and couldn't find him, he would

complain, "Where has that piccanin got to—somewhere off with a book, I bet. *Tengo*! Where are you?"

Tengo's mother sat at the kitchen table in the hour she had free between lunchtime and teatime and wrote a letter to her sister in Johannesburg.

> Tell your madam, once again, how grateful we are for the books she sent. Tell her the child is drinking up learning like the dry ground soaks up the rain. . . .

Tengo never mentioned the books to Frikkie because it shamed him now that even though the two of them were the same age, Frikkie was so much more advanced in schoolwork than he was. And since Frikkie never went inside their hut, he never saw the shelf of books.

Once, though, when they were both perched on branches in a gnarled old peach tree, picking the hard sweet fruit that would be cooked in syrup and stored in bottles in the pantry, Frikkie remarked as he munched on a peach, "My uncle told me someone sent you a box of books." Tengo nodded, reached up for a peach, bit into it, and said nothing.

Year after year Frikkie came to the farm—for the summer vacation in December, the winter vacation in July, the short midterm breaks. Year following year, the day after school closed for the holidays he was in his room in the farmhouse unpacking his suitcase. The two boys saw each other so frequently that neither noticed the change in the other—the bones in their faces growing heavier, their voices thickening, their hands growing large and their muscles harder and stronger.

The year they both turned thirteen, Frikkie arrived as usual for the July holidays. Even though it was mid-winter, the days were bright and hot with steady sunshine, the sky cloudless; but the night would drop down sudden and black and cold after the brief fiery sunset flared across the sky—and frost would crackle over the grass and a layer of ice harden on the water in the rain tank in the yard. By mid-morning it would all have melted.

The air was clear as glass and smelled sweet and pure, and the cry of the birds was sharp and bright as crystal. The water in the river was too cold for swimming, and the branches of the willows hung bare and yellow on the riverbank where the grass, dry now and prickly, clung to the boys' sweaters.

"There's going to be a big party for my uncle at the end of July," Frikkie told Tengo as they skimmed pebbles across the water. "A birthday party."

"How old will the oubaas be?" Tengo asked.

"Fifty. All my uncles and aunts and cousins are coming. My mother and father and sister will come and stay for the week. We're going to have a *braaivleis*. My uncle says he'll butcher an ox, and your mother is going to bake an enormous birthday cake so that we can put fifty candles on it."

"The oubaas is getting old," Tengo observed.

"When he dies," Frikkie said, "this whole farm will be mine. You can work for me and be my boss-boy."

Tengo picked up a heavy, flat, gray pebble from the riverbank, took aim at a tree stump on the opposite side, took a step back, and with an overarm swing threw the stone, hitting the tree stump dead center.

"Good shot," Frikkie said. He picked up a stone, aimed, threw, and missed. He sat down, leaning against the trunk of a willow, pulled a straw of dry grass, and chewed on it. "Will you, Tengo?"

"Will I what?"

"Will you be my boss-boy when this is my farm?"

Tengo, with perfect aim, hit the tree stump with a second stone. He stood for a few moments, looking down at Frikkie's hair, which was the same yellow as the willow branches, then turned and walked off.

"Hey—wait for me!" Frikkie shouted when, receiving no answer, he looked around and saw Tengo halfway up the slope. "Where are you going?" he asked as he caught up with him. "I'll get my soccer ball and we can have a game."

But Tengo went on, walking fast over the sere winter grass of the veld as if he had somewhere to go, as if he had received a message though he didn't know what the message was about.

Frikkie broke into a sprint to keep up with him. "Tengo, man! Where are you going?"

Swiftly, Tengo ran now, feeling the loping of his legs as they moved his body across the veld with the high blue sky over his head and the pure dry air pumping through his lungs.

"Oh, so you want to race, do you!" Frikkie called out. "Beat you to the gate then—"

But Tengo's feet felt as though they were skimming over the grass, scarcely touching it, as if the ground were streaming away under his feet; the wind rushed past his face, and he was filled with an urgency that impelled him swiftly—he did not know if it was away from something or toward something that he was running. Faster

he ran, and faster. He reached the gate long before
Frikkie.

The two boys leaned against the gate, panting, waiting
to get their breath back. Far off, over a distant *koppie*,
three vultures hovered, hanging in the air, motionless
almost, as though suspended from invisible strings. "They
can smell blood," Frikkie said. "Someone's out hunting.
Look at them—waiting until it's safe for them to drop
down and feast when the killing's over."

Oom Koos had been out hunting with some of the neigh-
boring farmers and had shot a large kudu buck. He had
butchered it and was working at the table under the
jacaranda tree, cutting up a haunch into strips to make
into *biltong*.

"Hey! I've been looking for you two *skellums*—where
were you? Loafing about when there's work to be done.
Come and give me a hand with the biltong."

He had filled a basin with coarse salt and spices, and
as he cut the strips of meat, he handed them to the boys
to rub with the salt mixture. "Make sure you rub it in
well," he warned them, "or else the meat will rot." Then
each salted strip had to be hooked onto S-shaped metal
hooks and hung from a wire that was stretched between
two branches of the tree where the sun and the wind
would dry them until they looked like stiff leather whips.

"Without biltong, Frikkie," his uncle told him
while they worked, "your ancestors—the Voortrekkers—
wouldn't have been able to survive the Great Trek. Dry
rusks, and biltong . . ." He felt Tengo's eyes on him and
looked up. "You don't know what the Great Trek is—
hey, Tengo?"

"No, Master," Tengo said. But he did know. He had read about it in one of the history books he had at the kraal. He pierced a hook through a strip of meat and hung it on the line.

"Tell him, Frikkie," the oubaas said.

"It was when our people—the Boers—all got in their covered wagons and trekked north away from the Cape of Good Hope."

"That's right, my boy. And when was it?"

"Oh, nearly a hundred and fifty years ago."

"And tell Tengo, why did they want to leave the Cape, Frik?"

"*Ach*, they wanted to get away from the English."

His uncle laughed. "Quite right. I'm glad you've been listening in class." His rough strong hands were covered in blood as he deftly cut the meat into even strips. The sharp knife blade glinted as it caught the sun. "The British were very hard on our people, the Afrikaner people," he went on. "They hanged some of them—just for whipping some kaffirs who had stolen their cattle. Then they forced them to free their slaves and told them they would pay them for their loss. *But* when the Boers came to collect their compensation, the British told them, 'Sorry, you have to take a ship and go six thousand miles over the sea to England if you want your money.' So all that money they had invested in buying slaves, they lost. They grew to hate the British—the way they favored savages, who weren't even Christians, over God-fearing Boers. So they decided to sell up—their farms, their furniture. . . . They packed what they needed into their covered wagons—salt and sugar and flour and seeds and plenty of gunpowder . . . their Bibles. And they packed their wives and children into the wagons, they took their

servants, and they drove their cattle and sheep along
beside them. They yoked in their oxen to draw the
wagons, and they set out—I can tell you it took a lot of
courage—and they made their way into part of Africa
where hardly any white men had set foot before. They
were the first settlers in this part of the country. And
your relatives were among them, Frikkie. And that was
how our family got this farm. We paid for it with our
blood. Did you know that?"

"Yes, Oom Koos, but it's more interesting the way you
tell it than when my history teacher drones on and on."

"You should listen, my child. Those Voortrekkers were
very brave people. They loved the land. And they paid a
bitter price for it. After they got away from the British,
then *your* people, Tengo, fought them, and tricked them,
and slaughtered them just like I've slaughtered this
buck."

"How did they trick them, Oom Koos?" Frikkie asked.

Tengo, rubbing salt into the meat, listened.

"How? The native chiefs would agree to sell land to
our people, make a bargain with them: 'Yes, you can
have so much and so much—from the river to the trees
will be all yours.' Then, after the Boers outspanned
their oxen and set all their cattle out to graze—maybe
even started planting and building houses—*down* would
come the *impi* hordes with their *assegais* and *knob-
kerries*, and slaughter them all, and steal their cattle.
There were terrible battles between the Boers and the
kaffirs. They outnumbered us, but their spears couldn't
stand up to our guns, and they paid a heavy price for
making bargains with us and not sticking to them."

"When will this biltong be ready to eat, Oom Koos?"
Frikkie asked.

His uncle, wiping his hands on a rag, tweaked Frikkie's ear. "So you're more interested in your stomach than in the history of your people," he reproached him.

"*Eina*! That hurt!" Frikkie rubbed his ear with the back of his wrist because his hands were covered with salt and blood. "*Tell me*, Oom Koos, when will it be ready? I love buck biltong."

"Skellum!" Oom Koos ruffled his nephew's fine yellow hair. "The weather's so dry, and there's a good breeze blowing, so it shouldn't take longer than two weeks."

"Two weeks! That's a long time to wait. We'll give Tengo a piece, won't we, Uncle, since he's helping us make it."

"I don't like biltong," Tengo said. "It's too dry and salty, and it tastes of blood."

The oubaas laughed. "All the more for us then," he said.

Tant Sannie came to the kitchen door and called out across the yard that lunch was on the table.

"We're coming," the oubaas shouted. "You stay here, Tengo." He handed Tengo a long switch he had cut from a tree. "Stay here and use this to chase off the flies when they try to settle on the meat. Here, Frikkie, take this basin to the kitchen and give it to Selina to wash." He carefully wiped the blood off the butcher knife, and they went indoors.

Tengo sat on the bench flicking the switch at the flies drawn there by the smell of the raw strips of meat. *Even though the oubaas is so strong and so rich and so clever,* he thought to himself, *he doesn't know everything. And he doesn't know that he doesn't know everything. . . .*

Tengo had been reading history books. There had been a second carton from the people in Johannesburg—

more advanced books. And from what he had read,
Tengo understood something that the oubaas didn't; and
that Frikkie didn't. He had realized from the history
books that the Boers couldn't understand that the Africans had no notion that land could be bought, or sold, or
bartered for beads or cooking pots or mirrors. Just as no
one could buy the sky or the rain or the sunlight, the
land was there for those who lived on it to graze their
cattle; for them, their herds of cattle were their most
valued possession, and the grassy plains and the rivers
were there for their beasts to feed and water on.

The Boers came along in their wagons and thought
the African chiefs were selling them the land. They
didn't know that they were being granted only the right
to graze their own cattle, even to plant crops—*but not to
own it*, to fence it in, to possess it for themselves from
then on. *It was two different ways of looking at the same
thing*, Tengo thought, as the flies buzzed in irritation
away from his switch. *It was two different sets of people,
each owning cattle and each wanting the same land for
pasture. We were here before them. But their guns were
more powerful than our spears. . . .*

He had been out hunting a few times with the oubaas.
He had seen how easy it was, from a distance, to take
aim, fire—and a great kudu buck a hundred yards away
drops and rolls onto its side. He had been alongside the
oubaas as he had pulled out his hunting knife and slit
open the steaming belly of the slain animal, to gut it.
He had looked up and seen the vultures hanging motionless against the blue, waiting to descend to feed on what
was left behind on the grassy plain.

The tribes, with their skin shields and assegais, had as
little chance against the guns of the Boers as the kudu

buck had against the rifle of the oubaas. The Boers hadn't understood the Africans, and the Africans hadn't understood the Boers.

Tengo's arm grew tired of waving the switch about. He decided he didn't care if the flies settled on the oubaas's biltong, and he sat, deep in thought, under the jacaranda tree, making connections in his mind that he had never been able to make before the boxes of books had come.

He remembered how, when he had been unpacking the first box of books, he had felt it held something magic for him. Perhaps the magic, he thought now, was in knowing—understanding certain things that Frikkie and the oubaas were ignorant of, which gave him a power over them that he hadn't had before, a power that lessened their hold on him. . . .

Once he had worked his way through the second box of books, he had hoped for another. Whenever he saw the oubaas unloading a likely-looking package from the truck, his heart would trip at the thought that it might be for him. But more than a year had passed, and there were no more books from Johannesburg. His mother was sure they would come. "Be patient," she had told him, "my sister's madam is a good woman. She won't forget about you." But Tengo was sure she had forgotten.

From the kitchen window a shout disturbed his thoughts. "Tengo, you lazy kaffir!" the oubaas roared. "You're not supposed to be sitting there dreaming. Chase those damned flies off my biltong!"

Tengo raised the switch, and a cloud of black flies lifted off the meat and buzzed away.

.   .   .

Frikkie loved the winter evenings on the farm. Selina would light a fire in the dining room, and when dinner was over and she had cleared the table, she would rake the ashes with a poker and pile glistening black lumps of coal on the hot embers. Frikkie would lie on the hearth rug watching the tongues of flame lick at the coals until they glowed red with heat. His aunt and uncle would sit on at the table, his aunt occupied with her sewing or knitting, his uncle working at the farm accounts. At home Frikkie read comic books, but Tant Sannie would not allow them in the farmhouse—"they fill children's heads full of rubbish," she said. There was a radio, but it was used only for listening to the news or the weather forecast. Sometimes, on Sundays, if they could not get to church in Doringkraal, they would listen to a radio *predikant* giving the sermon in Afrikaans. There was nothing to read in the house apart from the big old Bible that had been with the family in the ox wagon on the Great Trek, and a pile of farming magazines. Frikkie would lie on his stomach in front of the fire, poring over advertisements for combine harvesters, tractors, milking equipment, fertilizers, until it was time to go to bed.

He sighed with contentment; he didn't have to worry about homework or about his strict new teacher who caned the boys for the least little thing—like a few words spelled wrongly or coming in a minute late after break. There was nothing to worry about here. He watched the blue flames leaping over the surface of the coals. The fire shifted, and fine ash rained through the grate, the blue flames turning orange and crimson in the deep heat. He wondered when Tessie's calf would be born and hoped it would be a heifer that would yield as much milk as its mother.

In the kitchen Selina wrapped herself warmly in a thick winter coat that used to be the madam's. Luckily, they were both big women, so it fitted well. The washing up was done, every surface in the kitchen wiped down and tidy. She parceled the remains of a roast leg of lamb that madam had said she could take, and put it in her cracked black plastic shopping bag. There was enough meat on it for her mother to make a tasty stew for the family to eat with their mielie porridge. She wound a shawl around her head and shoulders, switched off the light, and stepped out into the biting cold night. There was no moon, and the sky was thick with stars. Tengo was learning many interesting things about the stars, but to her they seemed like bright lights twinkling through small holes in the darkness.

Where the farm road sloped down toward the stand of eucalyptus trees, she could see the faint glow of light from the kraal. As she came nearer, she could pick out the orange radiance of the brazier of hot red coal that kept their hut warm and sent comforting light spilling out of the two small windows. She walked a little faster through the silence of the African night toward her family.

Early in the morning, when Tengo's grandmother was lighting the breakfast fire, she heard Frikkie calling over the veld. "Tengo! Tengo!" And soon he came running across the kraal. "Lettie," he asked the old lady, "is Tengo up yet?"

Tengo appeared, rubbing his eyes in the doorway.

"Tengo! Tessie's calf was born last night! My uncle and I were up nearly the whole night, and the vet came. Tessie had a really bad time, but she's all right now."

Tengo's father came to the door. "Is it a heifer?"

"Oh, yes, Timothy. A beautiful little white heifer. Hurry up and get dressed, Tengo. I want to show it to you."

While he waited for Tengo, Frikkie picked up a small red clay bull from the outer window ledge. He held it carefully while he closely examined it. The old lady squatted at her iron cooking pot, stirring, stirring the thick white maize porridge. High up in the bluegum trees a bird whistled a tune on the clear frosty air and was answered by a series of warbling trills.

When Tengo came out of the hut, he noticed at once the clay bull in Frikkie's hand.

"This is one that you made?" Frikkie asked.

Tengo nodded.

"Have you made a lot of them?"

"Not so many."

"Tengo, will you give me this one?"

Tengo hesitated. He felt glad that his friend liked the little bull so well that he asked for it, but at the same time he felt a reluctance to let him have it—as if the clay animal was from a part of his life that he wanted to keep separate from his friendship with the white boy.

In the silence Frikkie waited, encountering a closed look on Tengo's face, almost as if they were strangers. "Please, Tengo . . ." he said.

The old lady stirred the porridge. Timothy came out of the hut, yawning, stretching.

"You can have it," Tengo said.

"Thanks." Frikkie sounded offhand to cover the relief he felt. It would have been a blow to him if Tengo hadn't wanted him to have it. But it was such a beautiful little bull—taut with strength, as if it were about to break into a run—that Frikkie was unable to hide his pleasure.

"I'll keep it in my room at the farm always, Tengo. I'll never take it back to town. Come on, man, stop dawdling! Let's go and see the new calf. Race you to the gate!"

"Tengo!" his granny was calling after him, "what about your breakfast!"

But the two boys were racing over the veld swiftly out of earshot, their feet leaving imprints on the thin crust of crackling rime that whitened the grass. Soon the sun rose a little higher in the sky and melted away the two parallel tracks that led from the kraal to the farmhouse.

That night, after Frikkie had gone to bed, his uncle closed up the big black book in which he kept account of everything that went on at the farm. He had just entered the birth of Tessie's new calf. Tant Sannie's needles clicked away as she knitted at the large gray wool socks her husband always wore.

"I wish you could have seen those two boys this morning when they came to see the calf," Oom Koos said. "Frikkie went down to the kraal to wake Tengo, he was so excited. They watched Tessie suckling her newborn calf. I tell you, Sannie, their faces—it nearly brought a lump to my throat—the faces of those two kids, black and white. It was as if they were witnessing a miracle." He shook his head and gazed into the fire.

Tant Sannie unrolled some wool, started a new row. "Well, those two have been playing together since they were about three years old, don't forget, Koos. They've both grown up on the farm. It's in their blood."

"He's a smart kaffir, that Tengo," Oom Koos remarked. "And a good worker. If he stays, in a few years time I could trust him to take care of the dairy. But—I don't

know. . . . Did you see that little clay bull he gave
Frikkie? I tell you, Sannie, that piccanin's too clever
for his own good."

His wife rolled up her knitting and put it away in
her workbasket. "These quiet kaffirs—" she remarked.
"They're the ones you have to watch. They don't say
much, but their thoughts—you never know what they're
thinking. It's time for bed, Koos. You were up most of
the night with Tessie's calf. You look tired."

C H A P T E R

6

*T*he last week of July was a frenzy of cooking and baking and preparation for Oom Koos's birthday party. Frikkie's parents and sister arrived. His mother and Tant Sannie and Selina were busy from early morning, roasting, grinding, chopping, rolling, stirring, stuffing sausage, pulling cakes and tarts and pies out of the furnace of the oven. The farm kitchen was filled all day with wonderful smells. Frikkie's father helped Oom Koos butcher the beef and hang strings of colored lights across the yard, and they drove into Doringkraal and came back with the truck loaded with crates of beer and brandy and colored soft drinks for the children.

Since his mother was so busy, Frikkie had to take care of his sister. He was used to having the freedom of the farm to himself and resented Sissie trailing about behind him when he helped in the dairy or rode on the combine, or when he and Tengo went down to the river or played soccer. She couldn't keep up with them when they ran, or catch a ball properly, and often the two boys would

try to run off without her. But she would come wailing
and protesting after them. Sometimes they got away
from her, and she would complain to the grown-ups and
Frikkie would be reprimanded.

She stood outside the fowl run, watching the boys
collect eggs. "I've got nothing to do," she said in a cross,
bored way.

"Come and help us," Frikkie said.

"No. I don't like chickens. They'll peck my legs."

"Why should they peck your legs when they've got
all this fowl food. You wouldn't taste good, even to a
chicken."

The boys laughed, and she stamped her foot and
shook the wire fencing. "I'm going to tell Ma that you
and Tengo are making fun of me," she shouted, and
flounced off back to the house.

Tengo was glad she had gone. He didn't care for
Sissie. She had a round pink face and light blue eyes,
and her hair was as pale as straw and pulled back from
her face and plaited in tight little pigtails. To him she
looked as if the color had been bleached out of her. She
turned red very quickly in the sun and always had to
wear a hat outdoors. She never spoke directly to Tengo.
"Tell him it's my turn," she'd say to Frikkie. "Tell him
to pick one for me . . . tell him it's over there. . . ." If
he handed her what she'd asked for, she didn't say
thank you. He was glad that she seldom came to the farm.

They took the basket of eggs back to the house, and
Tengo's mother asked him to put them in the pantry.
He put the basket down on the polished red stone floor
and looked around. He had never seen so much food.
Every shelf was laden. To keep the flies off, beaded net
covers were spread over great platters of raw steaks and
chops and the homemade sausages they called *boerewors*.

There were dishes of *bobotie*, spiced ground meat covered with a layer of cream sauce and decorated with a pattern of leaves picked from the lemon tree. There was *melktert*, delicate sweet custard tarts, and *koeksusters*, twists of pastry cooked golden in syrup—all dishes the Afrikaners cooked, Tengo knew, for feasts and celebrations. There was the large cake his mother had baked, iced with pink and white icing and decorated with small silver balls.

Frikkie came into the pantry, followed by Sissie.

"Not bad, hey, Tengo?" Frikkie remarked.

"It's a real feast," Tengo said.

"Tant Sannie says I can put the candles on the cake," Sissie boasted. "Fifty candles."

"Would you like a koeksuster, Tengo?" Frikkie asked.

"Oh, I'm going to tell Tant Sannie on you." Sissie ran back into the kitchen.

Tant Sannie appeared. "All right, you two, just one koeksuster each, and then everybody out of here. We've got plenty to do, and you children are getting under our feet."

The next day Frikkie and Tengo were free of Sissie. She had a fever and a sore throat and had to stay in bed. They did their jobs around the farm, and in the afternoon had a game of soccer, enjoying themselves without her.

They rested under the jacaranda tree, and Frikkie took a stick of biltong out of his pocket. "Want a piece?"

Tengo shook his head.

"Oh, I can't cut it. I must have left my pocket-knife in my room."

Just then Oom Koos called across the yard. "Frikkie, come and give me a hand with this pump."

"Coming, Oom Koos. Tengo, do me a favor. Go to my room and get my knife for me. I think I left it on the chest of drawers next to the bed."

Tengo went into the kitchen, told his mother where he was going, and went through into the main part of the house. He rarely went beyond the kitchen door. There was a long passage with the dining room on one side and the sitting room on the other. The sitting room door was open, and he peered in at the shiny furniture: the tightly upholstered chairs and sofa, small tables with vases and ornaments set on lace doilies, a glass-fronted cabinet with a china tea set in it. The room faced south and was cold and gloomy. His mother had told him it was used only when the minister came to tea.

The passage turned right, and he knew Frikkie's room was at the end of it. He passed by an open door and saw Sissie in bed.

In Frikkie's room, on the chest of drawers, the red clay bull was standing on a crocheted doily. Beside it was the penknife. He took it and went out of the room.

As he walked back down the passage, Sissie called out, "Tengo!"

He stopped in the doorway.

"Come in here."

He went in.

"What do you want in the house?"

"Frikkie asked me to fetch his penknife."

"You should say *Master* Frikkie."

He made no answer.

"Why can't he get his knife himself?"

"He's helping your uncle with the pump."

"What does he want it for?"

"To cut biltong."

"For both of you?"

"No."

"Why not?"

"I don't like biltong."

She was wearing a yellow nightgown. The bed was scattered with crayons she was using to color in a picture book.

"I want some biltong. Ask him to bring me a piece."

There were footsteps down the passage and the madam came into the room. "Tengo! What do you want here in the small madam's room?"

"He came to fetch Frikkie's knife," Sissie piped up.

"Well, if you've got it, take it and go. And don't let me catch you in here again, d'you hear!"

He turned and left. As he went down the passage he heard the madam saying in a sharp voice, "You must *never* let a kaffir boy into your room again, you silly girl. D'you understand me! You have to be careful."

Passing through the kitchen, he heard his mother say something to him, but he went right on and out the door without stopping.

Frikkie came across the yard. "Find my knife?"

Tengo handed it to him. "Next time get it yourself."

"What's wrong?"

Tengo said nothing. He wished Sissie hadn't come to the farm. He felt bewildered and sore inside. He wanted to get away from Frikkie—from all of them. He said he was going back to the kraal and left Frikkie cutting and chewing slices of biltong under the tree.

A cold wind had sprung up, and it came in through a hole in the elbow of his sweater. He felt chilly, but he roiled inside; he wondered how it was that he could be feeling shamed and sickened when he had done nothing wrong.

Outside the hut his grandmother was peeling vegetables for the evening meal. He sat down on the ground
beside her, leaning against the wall. She looked at him.
"Are you sick, my child?"

He shook his head.

"What is wrong then?"

"Nothing."

One by one she dropped the peeled vegetables into a
basin of water. The basin was chipped and rusted. *I've
seen that basin every day, since I was born,* Tengo
thought.

"Have you and the kleinbaas had a quarrel?"

He watched her deft, gnarled black fingers cut orange
rounds of carrot into the iron cooking pot. "No. But
Granny, I don't understand—I don't understand those
people up at the farm, how they think. . . ."

She took an onion from the basin, sliced it into rings.
"They won't be here forever, child. Once there was a
time without them. There will be a time without them
again. . . ."

On the Saturday of the party, Timothy and Tengo and
old Ezekiel, with a few of the others at the kraal who had
been asked to help, went early up to the house.

There were to be sixty guests. From midmorning the
cars came streaming up the farm road. One of the boys
was put in charge of the parking and directed the cars
to a field next to the sheep-dipping tanks.

Long tables had been placed under the jacaranda tree,
food and drinks set out; the old upright piano on which
Frikkie's mother and his aunts had practiced when they
were girls had been carried out into the yard by four of

the farm workers. Wood fires were lit in the barbecues, and when they burned white-hot, fat sausages were set spluttering and spitting with steaks and chops to sear over the flames. The bright sunny air quivered in waves above the cooking meats, and the savory smell drifted down to the kraal and drew the farm children up to the house. They gathered along the wire fence, chattering and staring, in their faded, tight, torn clothing, observing the festivities with curiosity. Some of the bigger children carried baby brothers or sisters tied to their backs in knotted blankets; the babies craned their small necks sideways to get a view of the goings-on.

Tandi had a cough that day and had to stay in bed, with her grandmother taking care of her; her mother had promised to bring back food for her from the party. She played with some dolls that had been handed on to her when Sissie's mother had made her clear out her toy cupboard.

Tengo was kept busy carrying out crates of soft drinks and dishes of food, clearing away dirty plates and bringing out clean ones. In the scullery old Ezekiel dried dishes as Selina handed them to him, the two of them laughing and discussing in their own language the ways of the white people.

When they could eat no more, and were wrestling and chasing one another and getting in everyone's way, Frikkie and a flock of his boy cousins were ordered by Oom Koos to go and play in the field beyond the yard. Frikkie came hurrying through the kitchen to fetch his soccer ball from his room; on the way out he ran into Tengo, who was coming in with a stack of dirty plates. "Nice party, hey, Tengo?" he called out as he sped through. "My cousins and I are going to have a game of soccer." Tengo handed the plates to old Ezekiel, who scraped them and passed them to Selina to plunge into the hot soapy water.

"Give us a hand with the drying, Tengo," his mother asked. He stood at the draining board with a dish towel in his hand, watching the bright noisy gathering through the window; beyond the yard he could see the boys kicking the ball around in the field.

When the sun began to slip down like a great red plate over the horizon, the strings of colored bulbs were switched on, and their light fell on the farm children peering through the fence so that their wondering faces glowed pink and green and gold in the gathering dusk. The birthday cake was brought out and a gasp went up from the guests when all of the candles had been lit by Sissie. Their flames danced and fluttered, illuminating the faces gathered around and throwing long grotesque shadows under the tree.

Oom Koos filled his huge chest with air, puffed out his cheeks, and a loud cheer rose up when, with one breath, he blew all the candles out. Watching through the kitchen window, old Ezekiel observed, "The oubaas is as strong as an ox."

The cake was cut and served, and coffee cups were filled from large steaming urns. Then the dancing began. Frikkie's mother sat down at the piano, pressed the loud pedal down as far as it would go, and the old Afrikaner folk tunes surged tinnily out of the ancient instrument. The dancers lined up in rows—men to one side, women to the other—and they wound and whirled and skipped and twirled their way through the traditional old folk dances—"Jan Pierewiet," "Ek soek my Dina," and the lively "Suikerbossie."

Sissie came in pink-cheeked and hot from the dancing and excitement, with two giggling girl cousins, each carrying a plate with a slice of birthday cake on it. "Ma says I have to have a rest, Selina. We're going to eat our cake in my room."

At that moment Frikkie dashed in with a milk jug in his hand. "My ma wants more milk for the coffee, Selina." In his haste he bumped into one of the girls, dropping the jug and knocking the plate out of her hand.

"Oh, *Frikkie* . . . Look what you've done!" Sissie exclaimed.

On the floor lay a mass of smashed crockery and squashed cake; pink and white icing was splattered over the linoleum and little silver balls scattered all about.

Tengo had been in the pantry stacking clean plates on the shelf when he heard the crash and tinkle of breaking china. He came to the pantry door and looked out to see what had happened.

"*Frikkie*, you're going to get it from Tant Sannie!" One of the cousins—a fat girl with short, straight-cut dark bangs—held her hand over her wide-open mouth and stared accusingly at Frikkie.

"Oh, it doesn't matter," the other cousin said. She was a thin, freckled girl of twelve, with a mass of red, frizzy hair. "The boy can clean it up." She turned to old Ezekiel. "Hey, boy—Jim—what's-your-name, come over here and wipe this mess up off the floor."

Tengo found that he had got from the pantry door to the middle of the kitchen without being aware he had moved. The shock of the girl's words had propelled him across the room as if he had been catapulted. He found himself standing in front of her, shaking with an intensity of hot rage that for a moment choked him and made it impossible for him to speak. He could not believe what his ears had heard—a strange girl addressing the respected old Ezekiel as if he were one of the stray farm dogs.

In a tight, low, terrible voice, Tengo spoke the words that came to him then. *"Don't you call that old man boy."* He took a step toward her. *"You have no respect!"* His voice rose as he felt pure anger surge through him. "Can't you see! He is one of the elders of our tribe—he is older than the oubaas—he is from the chief's family! *Who says you can talk to him like that—"* He lifted his hand as though to strike her, and his voice dropped as he hissed at her through clenched teeth. "Don't you *ever* call an old man *boy* again."

There was silence in the kitchen. From a leaky tap a falling drop dripped, dripped, dripped, plopping into the water in the sink. Tengo's mother stood still, filled with misgiving, her hands in the soapy water, watching over her shoulder what was happening. Old Ezekiel, facing them, wiped the plate in his hand over and over, turning it, dry and shiny, around and around in the dishcloth, a small painful smile on his face.

Tengo felt his heart lunge in his chest, pounding against his ribs and knocking his wind out so that it was hard for him to breathe. His mouth was dry, and he could hear himself panting. His fists were fiercely clenched and he stared at the girl.

Frikkie stood silent, baffled, shocked at the force of Tengo's anger.

The red-haired girl had drawn back, a look of fear and disbelief on her face. She had turned pale, and the freckles stood out against her blanched features. Now, in a sudden movement, she stuck her head forward on her thin neck. "Don't you *dare* talk to me like that"—

she spat her words out—"You're nothing but a cheeky kaffir—"

Selina hurried forward, her hands dripping. "Quiet, children. You mustn't quarrel. Don't make a fuss. It's nothing." She came between Tengo and the red-haired girl so that they each had to move back. "Girls, just go to Miss Sissie's room. Kleinbaas Frikkie, you go out and get another slice of cake for your cousin." With outspread arms she herded the girls to the door.

"*Tengo*, I'm going to tell my aunt you've been cheeky," Sissie called out over her shoulder, her face full of glee and malice. "I'm sure my uncle will *beat* you with his *sjambok*!" Giggling, she ran off down the passage.

Now Selina got down on her knees between the two boys and started to pick up the pieces of broken crockery. Tengo and Frikkie faced each other across the bent back of the black woman.

Tengo felt his head throbbing as though something wanted to fly out of his skull.

The look on his face frightened Frikkie; it was as if he didn't know Tengo, as if he were another person. "Tengo—" he said. "Don't worry. I'll tell them not to say anything to my aunt."

Tengo looked away from him.

"I'll go right now." Frikkie went out, down the passage to Sissie's room.

"Tengo?" His mother looked up at him from where she knelt cleaning up the mess.

But he could not look at her. He tugged off the tea towel tied around his waist, dropped it on the table, and walked out; he pushed past the dancers in the yard, past the jingling piano where a group had gathered around Frikkie's mother, all singing their Afrikaans

songs in unison; he went through the gate and past the
farm children peering through the fence, past the boy
cousins having a tug-of-war with a thick length of rope.
The night was falling over the veld, and a few stars
glimmered faintly in the sky. He walked on, over the hill,
until he came to the banks of the little river, and sat
down then, leaning against the trunk of a leafless willow
tree, his perplexity so painful to him that the inside of
his chest hurt. His heart felt as if a hoe had raked it
over. The night was still, but inside him there was
turmoil. He didn't have the words for what he was feeling. He sat beside the darkening water, cold and confused, as the deep night thickened around him.

In the kitchen old Ezekiel brought Selina a dustpan, and
she swept the crumbs and fragments of china into it.
Shamed by the behavior of the red-haired girl, both of
them avoided referring to it. With a damp rag she wiped
the linoleum clean. She straightened, pulled herself up,
sighed. "Something is troubling Tengo. He is not the way
he used to be." She felt tired. She had been up and working since dawn. "I worry about him." She moved heavily
back to the sink.

Old Ezekiel, drying plates, said, "He is not a child any
longer. And it hurts, Selina. It hurts to live in this world.
And this is what he is finding out. This is why he is
troubled."

Selina twisted the knob of the faucet angrily. "I wish
the oubaas would fix this tap. I don't know how many
times I've asked him already. This *drip drip drip* the
whole day is getting on my nerves."

·   ·   ·

Frikkie went down the passage into Sissie's room. The girls were sitting on the bed sharing the cake. The fat cousin looked up at him. "I thought you were bringing us some more cake."

"I've come to tell you that you'd better not say *one word* to Tant Sannie or Ma about what happened."

"Why not—he's nothing but a cheeky kaffir boy," the red-haired cousin said.

"And he raised his hand at her!" the fat girl said. "He deserves the sjambok."

"I'm asking you a favor." Frikkie said. "Don't say anything—to anyone. Please. I don't want him to get into trouble."

The red-haired girl tossed her head and shook her hair over her shoulder. "Oh all right. What do I care."

"*We'll* keep quiet," the other one said. "But what about Sissie? *She'll* tell."

"Sissie?"

"What?"

"Don't say anything to Ma. Or Tant Sannie."

"Why shouldn't I?"

"Because I'm asking."

"What will you give me if I don't?"

"Anything you like."

She stared at the ceiling, thinking, scooped some pink icing off the plate with her finger, and licked it. Then she looked up at her brother, sly. "All right. Will you give me that little clay bull on your chest of drawers?"

Frikkie wanted to hit her, but he clenched his fingers and said, "Anything except that."

"That's not fair. All right then"—a concealed smile pushed up her round cheeks, giving her a secretive look—"what about your giant purple and green marble?"

She knew it was the best marble in his collection. He felt his body flinch. He bit down hard on his teeth to steady himself. In his pockets his fists were tight. "Okay. You can have it. But you have to *promise* not to say anything."

"I promise."

He came up close to her, threatening. "Sissie, do you know what happens to people who break their promise?"

"Leave me alone, Frikkie," she wailed, backing away from him. "I *promise*. I *promise*."

The red-headed cousin was watching him. "Why are you making such a big thing of it? What do you care about that native boy? Are you a *kaffir-boetie* or something?"

The other two girls giggled.

Frikkie felt his face turning red and hot. He said, "I'm warning all of you—" and walked out of the room.

The Sunday after the party was the last day of Frikkie's holiday. He would be driving back home with his family after tea. In the morning everyone went to church in Doringkraal, and he had to go with them. As soon as they got back, he changed out of his Sunday clothes and ran down to the kraal to say good-bye to Tengo. He hadn't been able to find him last night when the servants were clearing up after the party.

Outside the hut Tengo's grandmother was sitting in the warm sunshine on a straw mat. Her lap was filled with tiny colored beads; with needle and thread she was weaving a beaded border around a circular piece of white netting, making covers to keep the flies off food. When she had made a quantity of them, she would go and sit by the roadside with them on Sunday afternoons, and passing motorists would stop and buy them from her.

"Hullo, Lettie. I've come to say good-bye to Tengo."

"Auw, Kleinbaas! You're going so soon." She slipped the beads along the needle onto a length of thread, then wove them into the scalloped pattern of the border.

"I've been here a whole month." He watched the design appearing under the gnarled black fingers. "You can thread those tiny beads and you don't even wear glasses, Lettie."

"Auw, Kleinbaas. But my eyes—they are not so strong anymore."

"Is Tengo inside?" he asked.

"No, Kleinbaas. Tengo is not here."

"D'you know where he is?"

"He is gone with his father and Tandi to visit their cousins on Meneer Van Rensburg's farm."

The neighbor's farm was two miles down the road. "When will they be back?" Frikkie asked, dismayed.

The old lady moistened the end of a thread in her mouth, held her needle up to the light, and stabbed the thread through the eye. She shrugged, intent on her pattern.

Tengo knew he was leaving today, yet he had gone off without seeing him. Frikkie liked things orderly and unchanging. It troubled him that he would have to leave without saying good-bye to Tengo. He wanted to tell him that he had given his best marble to protect him against Sissie's mischievous tongue. He scuffed the toe of his shoe in the dust, looked out past the bluegum trees at the place where the red sand road joined up with the main road that would take him back to the town, to school. "Tell Tengo I came to say good-bye, Lettie."

"Yes, Kleinbaas."

"Tell him I'll see him when I come for the short holidays in the spring."

"Yes, Kleinbaas."

"Good-bye, Lettie."

"Good-bye, Kleinbaas." Her needle, like a silver fish, darted in and out of the beads in her palm, sliding them along onto the thread. Intent on her work, she did not look up.

Frikkie walked slowly back, dragging his feet. Going up the slope of the road, he looked at the farmhouse sitting on the rise of the hill—long and low, the walls whitewashed under the red-painted corrugated iron roof. On the *stoep*—the front veranda that ran the length of the house—there were wicker chairs and an old swinging sofa on the red stone floor; the houseboy, on hands and knees with his can of red polish, was waxing it up to the high shine Tant Sannie insisted on—yesterday's guests had left it scuffed and dusty. There was a tangle of bougainvillea growing over one end of the stoep that in early summer would be a profusion of flowering purple. He always hated to leave the farm at the end of the holidays, hated to go back to school . . . spring was still a long time off. He liked things to stay the same . . . he didn't like change. . . .

When he got inside everyone was eating lunch, and his father was sharp with him for being late. After lunch there was a flurry of packing; the car had to be loaded up with eggs and butter and cream and biltong and a side of lamb and bottles of Tant Sannie's jams and preserves. There was no time to run down to the kraal.

After tea Tant Sannie hugged him, and Oom Koos put up his fists like a boxer and made a few playful jabs at

Frikkie's chest. "Don't look so *treurig*, old fellow—so mournful." He lifted Frikkie's chin with his great knuckled fist. "You're going back to school, not to jail."

"It's the same thing," Frikkie said, and everyone laughed.

Tant Sannie and Oom Koos stood on the stoep waving as long as the car was in sight. Frikkie and Sissie waved back until the turn where the farm road joined the main road and the farmhouse disappeared from their view. As the distance lengthened, Frikkie turned and kneeled, looking longingly out of the rear window. High on the hill he could see the single plume of smoke rising straight up into the blue from the farmhouse chimney; further down, along the slope of the valley, beside the eucalyptus trees, the haze hung blue-gray from the cooking fires and the coal braziers of the mud huts of the kraal. He wanted everything to stay the same . . . nothing to change. . . .

C H A P T E R

7

*A*fter Frikkie left, Tengo knew that he could not go
on the same way. There would have to be some change.
He did his work, but he was restless, dissatisfied. Usually
he missed Frikkie when he went back to school, but now,
even if Frikkie were still here, Tengo knew he would
avoid him. He hadn't wanted to see him after the night
of the party and had gone away on purpose.

He felt separated from everyone—from Frikkie, from
the white people up at the house, from his parents and
his kin at the kraal. He no longer enjoyed his work on
the farm. Even the books on the shelf, because he had
read them so often, had lost their interest for him. He
had given up hoping another box would come; he knew
that the people in Johannesburg had forgotten him.

He was quiet, moody. Many things he hadn't noticed
before angered him now. There was so much he needed
to understand, and no one to talk to about what troubled
him. His parents went along with the way things were.

They asked no questions, and they had no answers when he asked questions.

"Why can't you have your own farm?" he asked his father. "Why do you have to work all the time for the oubaas?"

His father chuckled. "A farm costs a lot of money, my boy. Where can a black man get money to buy his own farm?"

When his mother came into the hut one night after work and slumped on a low wooden chair beside the hot coal brazier, too tired to take off her coat and shoes, Tengo asked, "Mother, how old is the madam?"

"She and I are the same age, Tengo."

"Then why can't she serve the oubaas his supper and clear the table, so that you could leave earlier and come home and eat supper with us?"

His mother looked up at him, then into the fire. She warmed her hands in front of the hot red coals. "Don't ask questions that have no answer, my child. The main thing is to have work and have enough to eat and a place to live with a roof where we can all be together. Nothing else is important."

Tengo remained quiet. But he was sure that there *was* an answer to his question. And he was sure, as well, that there were other things that were important too.

When he was asleep, his mother said to his father, "I am worried about Tengo. He is changing. He is not happy anymore. Something is going on in his mind—it makes me feel anxious. He needs more books. He needs to study. I was sure that Matilda's madam would send more books, but it's been a long time now. . . ."

"He is a clever child, Selina. Perhaps we have to let him go away to school—"

"No!" she cried out. "Don't ask me to send him away, Timothy."

He patted her shoulder. "Well, we must be patient. At his age boys get restless. He'll settle down."

"That Tengo—" Oom Koos complained to his wife in late winter. They were sitting in front of the fire after dinner. "I had great hopes for him. But now, I don't know. . . . He's growing into one of those sullen kaffirs who doesn't look you in the eye when you talk to him."

"Is he getting cheeky?" Tant Sannie asked. She slipped a wooden darning egg into the heel of a sock, and with needle and yarn started to weave a neat patch over a hole Oom Koos had worn in the heel.

"No . . . He does everything he's supposed to do. But he used to be eager, willing—and now . . . I don't know what's got into him." He shook his head, stared into the fire. "These kaffirs—I tell you—you can live your whole life with them and still not know what goes on in their heads."

The spring brought a flush of green to the dry brown veld. Tight buds on the branches of the willows broke open into tiny yellow leaves, and from the hilltop the gleam of the river was banked up in pale gold. The fields of light green new corn stretched away to the horizon, the thornbushes turned green and new lambs skipped about, bleating pathetically if their mothers moved away from them.

Frikkie arrived for the short vacation. He visited all his favorite places and then went looking for Tengo. He found him sweeping out the cow stalls.

"Tengo! I'm here! I thought the school term would never end. Man, I tell you, it's a relief to get away from old Snake Steenkamp."

Tengo leaned on the broom. "Who's that?"

"My history teacher. Man, he is so *strict*. *Dates*! You have to know long lists of dates. When was the battle of Blood River? the Matabele Wars? the Jamieson Raid? the Boer War? And if you can't answer right away, *bang*! Down comes his cane on your hand. And *eina*!—it hurts. It's so boring having to learn all that dry old history. Oh, ten days away from old Snake—I can't believe it. I'm going to unpack. Call me when you're finished here and we can have a game of soccer before it gets dark."

Tengo went on sweeping. Blood River he had read about in a history book. But the Matabele Wars? He wondered as he worked—the Jamieson Raid . . . the Boer War . . . what were they about? They were stories that had really happened. He burned with the need to know. He felt his ignorance kept him as weak and powerless as the new lambs bleating after their mothers.

When he had cleaned out the last of the stalls, he put the broom away and took a shortcut across the veld back to the kraal. He didn't feel like playing soccer with Frikkie.

The ten days of Frikkie's vacation sped by, were over too soon. Somehow, he and Tengo didn't spend much time together. It was a busy time on the farm, and Frikkie was busy a good part of each day working with Oom Koos on the combine—spreading fertilizer, plowing, spraying.

"Can Tengo come on the combine with us?" he asked his uncle one morning.

"No. Kaffirs are no good with machinery," Oom Koos

answered. "They're good with animals, with donkey-
work. But give them a piece of machinery, and they
soon mess it up. Better to let them do what they're
meant for."

A couple of times the boys kicked the soccer ball about,
but Frikkie saw that Tengo wasn't really interested and
was making only halfhearted attempts to shoot goals
between the wash-line posts they had used as their goal
since they were small boys. When they were working
with the cows, Frikkie had looked up once to see Tengo
staring at him in an odd way. Tengo had looked away
quickly and gone on milking. The cup they often drank
raw milk from hung on its hook, and neither of them
suggested using it.

On the last day of the holiday they went down to the
river. Tengo was not exactly unfriendly, but he was
quiet and didn't seem to be listening when Frikkie
spoke. They skipped stones across the water, and Frikkie
was about to tell Tengo how he had bought Sissie's
secrecy with the best marble in his collection; but something put him off. He wasn't sure what it was—something
forbidding about Tengo these days—and he decided it
would be better not to talk about it.

"This holiday has gone so fast," he said instead. "When
I come back in the summer I'll be fourteen."

"So will I," said Tengo.

"Let's measure who's taller," Frikkie said.

They stood back to back and felt the tops of their
heads.

"That's no good," Tengo said. "Here—stand against
the trunk of the tree." He picked up a stick and rested
it on the top of Frikkie's head. Where it touched the tree,
he scratched a mark into the bark with a sharp stone.

"Now your turn." Frikkie measured Tengo and they

both stood back to inspect the marks on the tree. Frikkie's mark was about an inch higher than Tengo's. "Better eat more *mielie-pap* if you want to catch up with me," Frikkie teased him.

Tengo didn't laugh. When they parted at the gate, he said good-bye and walked off. Frikkie watched him as he went away down the farm road, in a tight navy sweater, his hands in the pockets of his khaki shorts, kicking a stone along the ground as he made his way into the valley.

"Tengo," he called out, "see you at Christmas. . . . *Good-bye . . . Tengo. . . .*" His voice echoed in the valley— ". . . bye . . . Tengo-o-o-o. . . ."

But Tengo didn't seem to hear him. He didn't turn around or wave; he walked on, kicking the stone as he went.

The young ears of corn in the plantation thickened and grew heavier; their silken tassels began to form; the new lambs and calves lost their babyish look; and the bougain-villea spilled purple over the stoep creating a cool shaded corner of shelter from the steady heat that blazed all day. The ground was parched. Every day Oom Koos came out and stood on the stoep that overlooked his vast farm. Every day he looked up at the sky hoping to see a cloud no bigger than his fist that might mean rain. But the December sky seemed to have been enameled over with a coat of impenetrable blue that no cloud could break through. Worried, he would shake his head and go in-doors to his breakfast.

In the afternoon Tant Sannie sat on the stoep in a wicker chair in the shade of the bougainvillea. Usually she took a nap after lunch, but in the intense heat her bedroom was too close and stuffy. She worked at her embroidery. She was making tray cloths for the sale of work to be held at the church before Christmas. The funds they raised were for the aid of poor whites whose plight the minister had described to the congregation. "We cannot allow our own Afrikaner people to live like kaffirs," he had told them. "We must come to the aid of our brothers and sisters who are less fortunate than we are. . . ." With a strand of red silk she worked a few flowers in lazy-daisy stitch, then looked up at the sky. All the farmers in the district were beginning to worry about the drought. If there were no rain soon, the mielie crops would be ruined; and the water in the dam was getting lower by the day, so that the cattle had to wade into the mud to drink. On Sunday at church the minister had prayed for rain.

From the kitchen there came a clatter and the sound of breaking crockery. Clicking her tongue with annoyance, Tant Sannie put down her sewing and went inside. Selina was sweeping shards of patterned china into the dustpan.

"Selina! That vegetable dish is from the dinner service that belonged to the master's grandmother! What's the matter with you, girl! Yesterday you broke a cup and on Friday you burned the bread!"

"Auw, Madam, I'm very sorry." She straightened up and emptied the fragments into the dustbin. "I don't know what's wrong with me lately. It's because my heart is sore . . . I have a lot of trouble."

"What's the matter, Selina?" madam asked sharply. "Why haven't you come and told me something's wrong."

"It's Tengo, Madam."

"Tengo! Is he up to no good? If he's in trouble with the law, we can't help you, you know."

"No, Madam. Tengo is a good boy. He wouldn't do anything wrong. No, Madam. He is driving us mad. He wants to go away from here—from the farm. He wants to go to school. That is all we hear from him, night and day, day and night."

"School! Why, isn't he happy on the farm? We treat him well. He has a full stomach."

"No, Madam. You and the oubaas, you are very kind. It's not that. He is a clever boy, and he has always wanted to learn, to study. But since my Zinsi went away to school and got sick and died—and that was not so long after we lost our baby—I am afraid to let him go."

"Why should you be afraid? The school at Boesmans-kloof isn't far. He could go there and come home at weekends."

"No, Madam. He doesn't want to go there. His cousins have told him it is a very poor school. He wants to go to school in Johannesburg."

"Johannesburg!" madam said. "The child must be mad. Does he have any idea what is going on there? The township is a terrible place—filthy and full of criminals. And now agitators are making trouble there all the time, stirring up unrest so that the police have to come in to try and quieten things down."

"I know, Madam," Selina said. She sighed deeply and shook her head. "Timothy and I, we are telling him this all the time . . . every day. But he says if his cousins—Joseph and the others—are managing to go to school there, he can too. Joseph is a very good student; he is getting ready to write his matriculation exam. And this is what Tengo wants also."

"So what are you going to do, Selina?"

"I have written to my sister in Johannesburg. She and my brother and his wife and his mother-in-law, they have a house in the township. I've written to ask if Tengo can come and stay with them and go to school. But oh, Madam—my heart, it is very heavy."

"The master is not going to be pleased to hear this, Selina. After all the expense, and the training Tengo has had on the farm. He's worried enough about the drought."

"I'm sorry, Madam."

"Do you want the master to try and talk some sense into Tengo?"

"It won't help, Madam. His mind is made up."

"Well—" She mopped her upper lip with her handkerchief. "I'm sorry for your trouble, Selina—but I don't want any more china smashed." She went back out onto the stoep, lowered her bulk into the creaking wicker chair, and took up her embroidery again, a look of displeasure on her flushed, heated face.

At dinner that evening Selina came into the dining room with a tray. She set it down on the sideboard and brought the dishes of food to the table. The oubaas took up the carving knife and steel and sharpened the blade edge. "So, Selina—" With precision his great thick-fingered hands carved thin slices of white meat off the chicken breast. "What's this nonsense I hear about Tengo wanting to go to school in Johannesburg?"

"It is so, Master. Timothy and I, we are very worried about letting him go, but it's no use. He says if we won't let him go, he'll go without our permission."

"Maybe a good hiding is what he needs to shake all that nonsense out of him."

Selina remained silent, the tray in her hand.

The madam served cabbage and boiled potatoes onto their plates.

"Has he ever been to the township, Selina?"

"No, Master. He has never been to Johannesburg."

The oubaas gave a short laugh. "Don't worry then. He'll give the place one look and come running back to the farm, I promise you. I wouldn't worry myself too much about him remaining there if I were you, Selina."

"Yes, Master." She went back to the kitchen.

Tant Sannie cut open a potato on her plate, waited for it to cool. "I knew it would come to no good when those boxes of books came." She speared a piece of potato onto her fork and blew on it. "Filling his head up with ideas not suitable for a kaffir . . ." She placed the potato in her mouth and exuded its heat through pursed lips. "He used to be a perfectly willing piccanin before that."

"So long as a native knows his place he'll be all right." Oom Koos laid a couple of slices of the brown meat he knew she loved on her plate. "But once he starts getting ideas, he no longer knows his place—and then you get trouble. That's the reason for all the unrest they're having in the townships. I tell you, Sannie, when I was a boy growing up here on the farm, you would never have heard of a kaffir wanting to read and write." He poured gravy from the sauce boat over his food.

"Selina is very upset. She keeps dropping things and breaking them and letting the food burn. Look, these potatoes are scorched. Maybe you should try and talk to Tengo, Koos."

He shook his head. "Once a kaffir makes up his mind, Sannie, that's that. Nothing can change him."

.   .   .

The cruel heat of the day relented a little as the evening darkened and stars glowed in the violet sky. Frogs piped their song in the half-empty dam, and the farm dogs lifted their muzzles and howled as the moon came lightly up over the bluegum trees. Timothy and Selina and the old grandmother sat outside the hut enjoying the cooler air of the night. Inside, Tengo and Tandi slept.

"All those books I got for him," Selina said. "I was so glad. I thought they would satisfy him and keep him beside us. . . ." She sighed.

"You thought it would make his thirst less," Timothy said. "But those books are like salt—they have only made him more thirsty."

"The books are taking him away from us," Selina said. "And he has taught Tandi to read and do sums. In a few years she will be wanting to go away too."

The old lady opened a small tin, pinched out some snuff between her thumb and forefinger, sniffed, and sneezed. "The calf leaves the cow," she said, "the lamb leaves the sheep. How can it be different with a child?" She snapped the tin shut and slipped it into the pocket of her long skirt.

Tengo was pouring milk from a bucket into one of the large metal milk cans when the oubaas came into the dairy. "So, Tengo. What's this I hear? I've spent all these years training you, teaching you, feeding you. And just when you're becoming useful to me, you're walking out on me. You're an ungrateful kaffir, that's what you are."

"No, Master. Master has been good to me. But I want to learn—to get an education."

"What for? What's wrong with the education you've

been getting from me? You stay on, and by the time you're eighteen you'll be a skilled agricultural worker. I pay my experienced boys good wages."

Tengo looked down at the ground. "I want to study things I can't learn on the farm."

"The problem with you is you're getting too big for your boots. Not only you—too many of your people as well. Stirring up mischief in this country. If the black people know their place, we can all get along together nicely in this land of ours. But once they start to overstep the mark—I tell you, Tengo, they're asking for trouble."

Tengo remained silent. He didn't understand what the oubaas meant. But he knew that the oubaas, and his parents as well, wanted to stand in his way, to block him from something that stirred in him and wouldn't leave him alone; something in him that wanted to know, that asked questions, that wouldn't let him be until he was in a place where he might find some of the answers.

"Well," the oubaas said, "if your mind's made up, there is nothing I can do. But you'll regret it, piccanin. And you'll come running home asking for your job back. Breathe this air here"—he inhaled, expanding his great chest—"clean, pure. . . . You'll remember the air, and the quietness here, once you're in the stink and dirt and noise of the city, I promise you. And you'll ask yourself, *Why didn't I listen to the oubaas?*" He turned and walked out of the dairy.

Selina's sister answered her letter.

> Since Tengo is a child with such a strong wish to go to school, it would be wrong to keep him on the farm. If you can manage to send a little money from

time to time, it will help with the extra expense on the household. The family in the township will take care of Tengo. But remember—it is a dangerous place to live. But he will get an education there. If he does well in his matriculation exam, he can go on to one of the black colleges and become a teacher or a minister even.

They should send a telegram letting her know when he would be arriving, she wrote. Unfortunately she would not be able to get off from work to meet him at the station. She gave exact directions for him to get to her employers' house. It would be easy for him to get there on the bus. He should come on a Friday. He could stay over with her, and on Sunday, her day off, she would take him out to the township. She sent warmest greetings to all the family.

Selina walked about for a few days with the letter in the pocket of her apron, needing to work up her strength to tell Tengo and to make the arrangements for his departure.

CHAPTER

8

*T*engo sat on the train and watched the countryside flash past the window—the rolling veld dotted with thornbushes; occasional windmills, their blades not stirring in the dry, windless air; cows drinking at muddy dams with white tick birds stalking importantly among them to pick the ticks out of their hides; great stretches of mielie plantations, tin roofs of farmhouses flashing in the glare of the sun; groups of mud huts with naked black children tumbling in the dust among chickens and kittens. When the train slowed down sometimes at a level crossing, black children would appear with outcupped palms yelling, "Penny, penny, penny." And from the windows of the coaches where the white people were, coins or oranges or buns were thrown and the children scrambled up the embankment to retrieve them.

Everything was dry, yellowed, baked; bare, stony riverbeds showed cracked and fissured by the drought. Above, the hard blue sky, like a bowl clapped over the land, held the heat shimmering in waves across veld and farmland.

Every now and again Tengo patted his shirt pocket for the reassuring crackle of the folded page with the directions to his auntie's place in Johannesburg. He had read it a dozen times—*out the main entrance of the station, turn left, half a block, the number twelve bus, ask the conductor to let you off at Winchester Drive.* . . . It wouldn't matter if he lost the paper; he knew the directions by heart. He felt nervous, but at the same time his heart seemed to be rushing—like the train—with joy toward something he so longed for that he had made himself almost ill thinking he might never get to it.

He was relieved that his mother hadn't come to the station; it would have made it too hard for him. For the last week she had gone about so heavy and quiet that he wished he could tell her, *I've changed my mind—I'll stay—I'll stay*, just to see her stop looking that way. But he could not say it. He had to go.

In the morning, when he was packing his few things into a small cardboard suitcase, his grandmother had given him some beaded net doilies to take as presents for his relatives. "Give one also to Matilda's madam," she had told him. He had packed in, as well, a few of his clay animals. He hadn't wanted to, but his mother said his cousins might like them as presents. Watching him wrap them in crumpled newspaper and stuff them among his clothes, Tandi had asked, "When will you come back, Tengo?"

"Oh," he said, feeling grand, "I'll come home for the school holidays."

"Like Kleinbaas Frikkie?"

"That's right."

"When are the holidays?"

"He has not started school yet," their grandmother said, "and you're already asking when the holidays are."

"My friend Dimasala told me there are a lot of tsotsis in the township and they are very *bad*," Tandi said.

"I'll watch out for them. Here, Tandi, you can have this." He gave her a clay calf with its head uplifted as if it were looking for its mother. But Tandi still looked as if she didn't want him to go. "I'll write you letters," he promised. "And you must answer. It will be good practice for your handwriting."

"I wish you would stay, Tengo," she said. She was a thin, sickly child, always coughing, and when Tengo saw her large, deep-set eyes on him, he felt bad to be leaving.

"I must go, Tandi. Now you can sleep in my bed. You won't have to share the bed with granny anymore."

From Doringkraal the train went through to Johannesburg, so Tengo did not have to change. It was a mixed freight and passenger train that stopped at every small station along the way. His mother had given him a packet of sandwiches and a plastic bottle of sweet, milky tea. He had said good-bye to his parents in the driveway at the farm. His father had put the suitcase in the back of the truck and Tengo climbed up into the front seat beside the oubaas. He was glad that his mother had not cried when she hugged him before he got into the truck. They stood in the driveway in front of the house, waving, and he waved back, hanging out of the window until the road curved and he could no longer see them.

Timothy had looked at his wife then, concerned; but she only said, "I must go and peel the vegetables for lunch," and he watched her walk slowly and heavily back to the farmhouse kitchen. Then he went off to the dairy to sterilize the milk cans.

Tengo's parents had given him money to buy his train ticket, but when they got to the station and he reached into his pocket, the oubaas had said, "Keep your money, Tengo. You'll need plenty where you're going." The oubaas had bought him his ticket from old Meneer Viljoen, the stationmaster. "Here, put it in your pocket and don't lose it," he told him, "and here's a *bonsella* for you though you don't deserve it." He handed him a five-rand note.

Before taking the ticket and money Tengo put the palms of his hands together to show his thanks, and then cupped them to accept the gift. "Thank you, Master," he said.

The train came in. In front were the coaches for the white people—with upholstered seats, Tengo saw, like the sofas in the sitting room at the farmhouse. Then there were the freight cars, and at the back the third-class coaches for blacks, with slatted wooden seats.

"Get in, get in," Meneer Viljoen told him. "Don't stand there staring like a donkey."

Tengo got in and the stationmaster slammed the door shut. There was no one else in the carriage, and Tengo put his suitcase on the metal rack above the seat and leaned out the window. The train smelled of coal dust and metal. Outside on the platform the oubaas and Meneer Viljoen were laughing and talking and lighting up cigarettes. Tengo clutched the ledge of the window, hardly believing that he really was on a train.

Then suddenly Meneer Viljoen looked at his watch, blew his whistle, took a green flag from his pocket and waved it. The oubaas shouted, "You're off—*totsiens*, Tengo—see you!" And the train chugged out of the station and away from Doringkraal.

Tengo lifted his hand to wave. His mouth was dry and his heart raced with excitement. He thought, *The train is going so slowly I could still jump out.* But then it picked up speed, the little red-roofed station fell behind, and only the endless veld was all around. He sat down, leaned back, and watched the countryside rush past the windows.

At the station in Johannesburg there were more people than Tengo had ever seen. A man who had got onto the train at the station after Doringkraal told Tengo that he would show him where to get his bus. He was almost as old as Tengo's father; he told Tengo that he worked in a supermarket in Johannesburg and had been home to his kraal to visit his wife who had had a new baby. The baby was already six months old, but he had not been able to take leave until now because they had already given him time off for his father's funeral. He could have taken leave without pay, but since the new baby was his fifth child, he could not afford to give up the money.

Tengo gave the man one of his sandwiches, and they shared the bottle of tea, which was only lukewarm but still refreshing. Later, when the train made a long stop at a station, the man got out and came back with a bottle of orange soda for each of them. He had asked Tengo if he wouldn't like to get off the train and stretch his legs, but Tengo was afraid that the train might go off without him, and stayed on.

Now he followed the man through the crush of people

and the clatter and noise of the huge station, out onto the street. The man laughed when he saw how Tengo stared open-mouthed at the crowded sidewalks and the high buildings and the traffic clogging the street, honking and filling the air with a roaring sound.

They turned left, and halfway along the block the man showed Tengo the bus stop, shook hands with him and wished him good luck with his studies, and disappeared into the throng.

A large clock in a shop window showed five. People were going home from work. They streamed into the station through separate entrances for blacks and whites and formed long lines at bus stops. The air smelled of gasoline, and the din drummed in Tengo's ears. Double-decker red-and-white buses stopped frequently to pick up white passengers. At the black bus stops the lines were longer, and the single-decker buses, when they came, filled up so that people were packed upright in them, with many clinging precariously to the outside platform. Tengo figured out that the overcrowded buses must be taking workers back to the townships beyond the city, because when the number twelve bus to the suburbs arrived, it was half empty.

He climbed on and sat down with his suitcase beside him. He told the conductor where he was going, and the conductor took his money, punched a ticket for him, and said he would call Tengo when they reached his stop.

Tengo patted the note in his pocket:

Get off at Winchester Drive—cross at the traffic light to the other side of the street—pass the shopping center where there are tables with yellow umbrellas set around the fountain—continue five blocks along

Winchester Drive to number 77—a high white wall
with big gates and a brass plate with Dr. Miller on
it. . . .

The city was left behind, and Tengo gazed, full of
wonder, at the beautiful houses and gardens of the suburbs. The bus stopped at a red light outside a school,
where boys wearing blue blazers and caps and long gray
trousers were walking away or riding off on bicycles. On
a green playing field marked out with white lines, boys
in white clothes were standing about, and a group in
blue uniforms were sitting on benches, watching. Tengo
saw one of the boys on the field bowl an overarm ball
and another strike at it with a bat and start running,
while a third ran along the field after the flying ball. As
the bus pulled away he realized that it was a game of
cricket being played. The wooden posts at each end of
the green must be the wickets the bowler was meant to
try and knock down. For years he and Frikkie had played
cricket in the yard at the farm, and many times Frikkie
had described how the game was supposed to be played
with eleven people on each team and the wickets on opposite sides of the field. Yet somehow, those white figures
dotted about on the green . . . he had never imagined it
would look that way.

"Winchester Drive," the conductor called out. His suitcase clutched in his hand, Tengo got off the bus. Following the directions he had memorized, he arrived at
number 77. The gates were closed. Through them Tengo
could see a tall house that looked as if one house had
been set on top of another, with a red tiled roof, at the
end of a long curving driveway. He saw smooth green
lawns bordered with flowers.

A black man in khaki clothes was on his knees in a flowerbed. "*Dumela*," Tengo called out.

The man looked up. "Dumela."

"I have come to see my auntie."

"Auw, yes. Come in. Open the gate and come in. Your auntie is waiting for you."

Tengo unlatched the gate and went in, latching it carefully as he had been taught to do on the farm.

"You've just come on the train?"

Tengo nodded.

"Go on up the drive, round the side of the house to the yard, and you will see the back door. You'll find your auntie in the kitchen."

Behind a high wire fence he saw two white girls in short white skirts running about on a red clay surface knocking a ball over a net to one another. There was a big square pool filled with green water, with white tables and chairs and bright umbrellas set about it. Around the side of the house three cars were parked. He came to a paved yard with a wash-line full of clothes and a jacaranda tree, just like the one at the farm, in full bloom. The back door was wide open. He knocked, and in less than a moment, it seemed, he was folded against his auntie's large bosom.

"Tengo! It is you! I have not seen you since you were a small boy. Look at you! You are just like your father."

"And you are like my mother," he said shyly.

"Come in. Come in." She took him into a white, smooth kitchen filled with white, smooth machinery. At an ironing board a young black woman was ironing clothes. "Dora. Here he is. My sister's child has come. This is Tengo."

She smiled at him. "Hauw—dumela, Tengo."

"He looks just like his father. You will be tall and thin. Sit down. Sit down. You're hungry, I'm sure, after that long train journey. Your cousin Joseph has been asking when you will get here." She sat him at a smooth white table and gave him a mug of tea and a plate of sandwiches filled with cold meat, and an orange. While he ate, she talked, asked questions, told him plans. He was to sleep on a mattress on the floor of the gardener's room, and on Sunday she would take him out to the township.

When he had eaten, she told him he looked hot and tired, and she took him to the servants' quarters and showed him how to take a shower. He stood under the cold, stinging needles of water for a long time. The farm, the kraal, the oubaas, Frikkie . . . it all seemed like a dream he had dreamed in another life.

That night, on the mattress on the floor in the gardener's room, he fell asleep while the gardener was still talking to him.

On Saturday morning Tengo ate breakfast early, before the family woke. Dora showed him everything in the kitchen and explained how all the smooth, white machines worked—a clothes washing machine, a dishwashing machine, a machine for mixing food and one for chopping food and one for toasting bread—even an electric knife for slicing meat. He watched her put a load of laundry into one machine and saw the clothes whirling around in suds behind a round glass window. At the farm there was an old washing machine with a wringer on top—nothing like this. He wished his granny could see it; she washed their clothes on a flat stone by the river.

His auntie was at the sink washing dishes. "Why don't you let the machine do the dishes for you?" he asked her.

"Oh, we never touch the dishwasher," she said. "It's not for us. It's for the madam to use when we're not here, on our days off."

"But then why is Dora allowed to use the clothes-washing machine?"

Dora laughed. "They never do their own laundry," she said.

Later, he met the Miller family when they came down to breakfast. There were two girls and two boys at home; his auntie had told him that the oldest son was away studying in England. They were all friendly when they saw Tengo in the kitchen, the parents and children asking him about his plans. He gave Mrs. Miller the beaded doily his granny had sent. She thanked him and said, "Matilda, put this in the drawer in the pantry."

"It was you I sent the books to, wasn't it?" she asked.

"Yes, Madam. Thank you, Madam." He thought she was going to explain why she had stopped sending them, but she said nothing more about them.

"Now you want to go to school and study seriously?" Dr. Miller asked.

"Yes, Master."

"Good for you, Tengo," Mrs. Miller said. "I'm sure you'll do well. If we can help you in any way, feel free to ask us."

"You'll need money for books," Dr. Miller said. "You must tell Matilda how much it comes to, and we'll let you have it."

"Hau, Master is very kind," Matilda said.

Claire, the older daughter, whom he had seen the day before playing what he had learned from the gardener was tennis, wound a strand of her long dark hair around her finger. His auntie had said she was fifteen. She was eating a piece of buttered toast. "This is a wonderful country," she said. "*He* has to pay for school and schoolbooks, and I get it all for free. How much longer can it go on like this?" she asked, seeming to address the light fixture above the table.

Tengo was surprised; here was a white girl asking the very question that had disturbed him for so long. She was receiving free education and yet was asking why blacks had to *pay* for theirs. Here was another new thing, another new idea for him to think about.

"Change is coming, change is coming," Dr. Miller said. "Meanwhile my waiting room is filling up with patients. See you all later." He went out to his car and drove away.

Matilda had brought some of Tengo's clay figures into the kitchen to show her employers. They were lined up on the windowsill—some cows, a bull with its head lowered as if it were about to charge, four oxen, and a thin, sad-looking farm dog in yellow clay.

"You made these on your own, Tengo? No one showed you how? They're good," Mrs. Miller said. "Very good. You should take art at school."

Tengo nodded, not knowing what that meant—*take art.* . . .

Later in the morning he helped Dora polish the silver. She told him it was done every week if it needed it or not. The table under the tree in the yard was spread with knives and forks and spoons, a silver tea set and coffee set, a silver soup tureen and ladle, silver trays. Dora spread each piece with a liquid that dried in a chalky layer, then rubbed with a soft cloth until she had worked up a bright gleam. She gave Tengo a cloth, and he enjoyed seeing the silver surfaces emerge, flawlessly reflecting the green leaves and the mauve jacaranda flowers.

He polished the soup ladle and was amused by the sight of his face swimming upside down and distorted in the shiny bowl, as if it had been scooped up from some strange soup. Claire came out through the kitchen door dressed in a bathing suit and carrying a pile of books and papers. She came over to the table.

"Tengo, I've been looking at your sculptures—"

"What is that, Madam?" he asked.

"Those clay animals you've made. They're really very good, you know."

"Thank you, Madam."

"Don't call me madam. I'm Claire."

"Yes, Madam," he said, then felt embarrassed when the other two laughed.

"Seriously, though, Tengo. You're gifted. You should study art."

"I don't know what that is—study art. . . ."

"Art—art is drawing, and painting, and those figures you make of clay. Wait a minute." She put down her load and went inside, and after a while came out carrying some large books, bigger than any Tengo had seen. "Look. These are art books. These are some of the greatest artists who have ever lived. Look—this is Rembrandt . . . this is Van Gogh . . . this is Michelangelo—he was a sculptor; he made figures, like you do, but out of marble. Look—aren't they marvelous? Here, look through them; you'll see what art is." She took up her books and papers, "I have to go and study now; I've got exams next week."

She went off to the swimming pool, lay down on the grass, and opened her books.

Tengo put down the silver ladle and the cloth and started to turn the pages of one of the art books. After some time had passed, Dora said, "I see I am going to have to finish all the polishing by myself," but he didn't even look up. He was studying each page in detail before turning to the next. The paper on which the pictures were printed was smooth and heavy, like the cream that ran off the milk in the separator in the dairy. There was so much to look at on each page that he was reluctant to leave it, but his greed for more kept him turning, turning the pages. Who was this? A holy man maybe—a figure of an old man with a beard, and horns on his head like the ones he had made on the bull, and a look on his face as if some terrible thing had happened. . . . Marble, she'd said it was made of, but this didn't look like the same stuff Frikkie's marbles were made of.

Dora finished buffing the knives and forks and spoons; she put them into a flat wooden box lined with green baize and took them inside. She came back for the rest of the silver, but Tengo hardly noticed she had gone. In the short time since he had left the farm, a whole new world had opened to him, full of strange and unexpected things. But nothing, it seemed to him, as wonderful, as amazing, as the paintings and the sculptures on the pages of the art books. He pored over them, intent, turning the pages, taking them in. . . .

Sometimes at the farm, at sunset or when the moon came up over the dark silent veld, he would be filled with a sense of how mysterious and beautiful the world was. Turning the pages, he was stirred now by that same feeling; he recognized it while not knowing what it was that he felt.

After supper that night he left the art books on the kitchen table. Before he fell asleep on the mattress on the floor of the gardener's room, the colors and figures from their pages flashed again and again behind his closed eyes and worked their way into his dreams.

On Sunday morning he had breakfast early with his auntie. She prepared food for the family's lunch and supper, and after she had served them their breakfast, she changed out of her overall and apron into her Sunday clothes, and the two of them set out for the township.

CHAPTER

9

A few days before the start of the Christmas holidays Oom Koos phoned to say that Meneer Van Rensburg, his neighbor on the next farm, was going to be in town visiting his sister. He would be driving back on the last day of school, and if Frikkie could be ready to leave by lunchtime that day, he would give him a lift to the farm.

Frikkie received permission to leave school early. When his teacher handed him his report card he said, "I wish you could be as enthusiastic about your schoolwork as you are about going to your uncle's farm, Frederiek." But since he had passed all his exams, it didn't bother Frikkie that his grades were not too good. He knew he could be a good farmer even though he didn't do well in history or geometry or science.

He was ready and waiting at the gate when Meneer Van Rensburg came by to fetch him, and he enjoyed the drive and the conversation about the drought and milk yield and mielie crops and the new bull Meneer Van

Rensburg had paid a lot of money for that he hoped was going to improve his stock of beef cattle.

"Drop me at the bottom of the farm road," Frikkie said when they reached the farm. "My bag isn't heavy. Thank you very much for the ride, Meneer."

It was a hot, still afternoon. The cicadas were sawing busily away with their hind legs, and the air was alive with their chirping. Frikkie's heart was filled with happiness at the thought of six full weeks on the farm—no school—no Snake Steenkamp to make his life miserable. A narrow track at the side of the farm road led through the bush to the kraal, and he decided he would cut through that way and stop by and see if Tengo was there.

One of the half-wild yellow dogs set up a snarling and yapping at Frikkie's approach. He picked up a stone and threw it, and the mangy creature ran off into the bush. There was no one about. The kraal seemed deserted in the bright flat sunshine. Even old Lettie was nowhere to be seen. The chickens huddled in what shade they could find. Frikkie put his suitcase down outside the hut and peered in through the doorway. After the glare outside, the circular interior was dim, and it took a few moments for his eyes to adjust to the change. He stepped in. The hut was sparsely furnished and spotless, the packed mud floor clean-swept. Faded flowered curtains that he remembered from his aunt's sitting room were strung up to divide the room into partitions, and in one of them old Lettie lay asleep on an iron cot. The room was impregnated with the smell of smoky fires and the sour odor of fermented maize porridge.

Frikkie was surprised to see a shelf crowded with books. He was about to step forward to see what sort of books they were when the old lady stirred, opened her eyes, and sat up.

"Oh, it is the kleinbaas." She swung her legs in her long dark skirt over the side of the bed.

"Hullo, Lettie. I didn't mean to wake you. I'm looking for Tengo."

"Tengo." She yawned. "He is not here."

"Is he up at the farm?"

"No, Kleinbaas. He is not here. He is away."

Old Lettie is still half asleep, Frikkie thought. "I can see he's not here, Lettie. When will he be home?"

"We do not know, Kleinbaas. Two years . . . three years maybe . . ."

"*Lettie.* What are you talking about? Where *is* he?"

"Tengo is gone away. To Johannesburg."

"Johannesburg! What for?"

"He is going to school there."

"School! When did he go?"

She shrugged. "Three weeks . . . four weeks . . ."

"But it's holidays now, Lettie. There's no school."

She got off the bed, padded barefoot across the earth floor, took up a bowl of sour porridge, and went out.

Frikkie followed her outdoors. The sunshine was blinding after the subdued light in the hut. "Will he come home for the holidays, Lettie?"

She was squatting now, breaking twigs for kindling to light her fire, and made no answer.

Frikkie picked up his suitcase and walked slowly away from the kraal. A little girl with her baby brother tied in a blanket to her back passed him and called out dumela, but he took no notice of them. He didn't believe that Tengo had gone away to school. He had never spoken of doing such a thing. Old Lettie must be getting a bit soft in the head. She was probably about a hundred years old by now and didn't know what was going on.

But she had spoiled his good mood. He made his way

up the farm road, his bag feeling heavier with every step, and went around the back of the house into the kitchen. Selina was at the sink scouring a pot.

"Kleinbaas Frikkie! Where have you jumped from?"

"I got a lift with Meneer Van Rensburg. He dropped me at the lower gate." He put down his bag and rubbed his hot damp palm where the handle had bitten into it. "Selina, I stopped off at the kraal to look for Tengo, and Lettie says he's gone to Johannesburg."

"That's right, Kleinbaas."

"But Selina, *why?*"

She rinsed the pot under a gush of hot water and set it on the draining board. "To go to school. Tengo has been wanting for a long time to go to school. He wants an education. We tried to keep him here with us as long as we could. Then he decided he must go." She shrugged. "And we could not stop him."

"I never knew . . . he never told me. . . . What school?"

"A school in the township. He is a very clever boy, Tengo. Learning comes easily to him." She sighed, filled the teakettle, and put it on the stove to boil.

"But Selina, it's school holidays now. Will he come home?"

"No, Kleinbaas. The minister at the Methodist church where my sister goes, he has arranged for Tengo to have extra lessons so he can catch up with the other students. He must study right through the holidays."

"Where does he live?"

"In the township with my sister's family. Tengo has many cousins there."

"But Selina . . ." He picked up his suitcase, feeling the sense of powerlessness that overwhelmed him at school when he got caned for not knowing his history dates by heart or when he had to stay in after school because his algebra answers were all wrong. This was a feeling he connected with school. He was always free of it at the farm. Here everything was always as he wanted it. And now—Tengo had gone. . . . It was all spoiled.

"Leave your bag, Kleinbaas. I'll put it in your room for you when I've made the tea; you look hot and tired."

"Where's my auntie?" he asked.

"In the dining room." Selina set cups and saucers on the tray, filled the milk jug, and plodded into the pantry to get the cake tin.

Tant Sannie got up from her sewing machine to hug Frikkie. "How was the ride with Meneer Van Rensburg?" she asked him.

"It was all right. Tant Sannie, did you know Tengo had been planning to leave the farm and go to school?"

She clicked her tongue with irritation. "I'm telling you, Frikkie, you get nothing but aggravation from these kaffirs. Here your uncle is spending time training him to be a skilled farm worker, and he takes it into his head he must have an education. Education! What good is education to a kaffir? It just fills his head with ideas he's better off without." She pedaled the treadle of her sewing machine and angrily seamed a length of fabric. She tore the thread free and folded up her sewing. "I tell you, Frik, they're getting out of hand these days. They used to be obedient, grateful—but now . . ." She shook her head, her face grim. "Now they're out to make trouble— for themselves and for us. Your uncle isn't pleased with the way things are going with the blacks in this country. He says we're going to have to show a strong hand to keep them under control."

"But Tengo . . . he's *always* been here."

Tant Sannie laughed. "Look at you, Frik. You look as if you've lost a ten-rand note. It's just one more ungrateful kaffir gone. They're all one lot; there's no need to look so mournful." She clapped the cover onto her sewing machine. "Your uncle will be coming in for his tea in a few minutes. He's very worried about the drought. Go and put your things away and have a wash now. Selina has baked your favorite fruitcake for you."

Frikkie went off to his room. He kneeled on the bed and looked through the window at the maize fields rolling away, the leaves yellowish-green and the stalks stunted by lack of rain. To the west there was a view of the gentle slope of the valley, the veld brown and dried out; he could see the stand of eucalyptus trees, with the smoke from the kraal drifting up into the cloudless blue. He turned and sat on the bed, looking around the room at all the familiar things, just as they should be, nothing out of place. On top of the chest of drawers the small clay bull stood on the crocheted doily. He went over and picked it up. Under his thumb the taut muscle of the haunches swelled; above the curly forelocks on its brow the small stumps of horn rose, pressing against his finger.

He wanted everything unchanged, continuing the way it always had been. And now Tengo had gone, without even telling him. . . . He was used to Tengo. They'd been friends since they were little kids. And now he'd gone away to school without ever telling him that that was what he wanted. The farm wouldn't seem the same place with Tengo not here. Why did he have to go? He pressed his finger down on the horns of the little red bull and they dug into his flesh.

"Frikkie!" His aunt's voice rang down the passage. "What's keeping you, child! Oom Koos is waiting for you. Tea is on the table!"

He put the clay animal down and went to wash his hands.

After tea his uncle asked him to come and help with the milking.

"I—I haven't unpacked yet," he said. "And—I've got a bit of a headache. I think I'll lie down for a while."

Tant Sannie felt his forehead. "You're not getting sick are you, Frikkie? I wondered why you had only one slice of cake. You should have let Meneer Van Rensburg bring you all the way up to the house instead of lugging a heavy bag over the veld in all this heat. Go and lie down, my boy. If you don't feel like getting up, Selina will bring you your supper in bed."

PART TWO

CHAPTER
10

*T*engo hardly noticed the noise and the smells and the dirt any more. After almost three years of living in the township he had become used to it. In the early days, though, in the shock of the crowdedness and the clamor, the absence of privacy, the everyday violence and tension and ugliness, he had lain awake in the night, thinking, *The oubaas is right . . . the oubaas is right . . . I can't take it . . . I have to leave this place and go back to the farm. . . .*

But he knew it was the open veld he longed for when he thought of the farm, with the high sky above it and the clean smell of the air and the warm breath of the cows. When he remembered the emptiness, the boredom, the unanswered questions that came to him from everywhere—from the stars and the insects and the flash and dart of the schools of small fish in the river, from the way the oubaas and his wife talked to his parents and the way his parents submitted to their lot—when he remembered all that, he felt his good fortune in escaping from there.

He rarely thought about Frikkie. Under the pall of smog, with the press and noise of township life, those days by the river—climbing trees, racing over the veld— seemed like a dream scarcely remembered after waking.

He no longer missed his parents and Tandi and his grandmother so much, or the comforting familiarity of the smell of smoke combined with sour porridge that permeated the inside of the round mud hut. Or rather, he thought, he had grown used to missing them. He hadn't been back to the farm since the day the oubaas had put him on the train. In the school holidays he had to study hard to catch up with all the years of schooling he had missed.

He had looked forward, when he came to live in the township, to being able to spend time with his cousin Joseph. But Joseph was away from home a good deal, and Tengo rarely saw him.

He was lucky that Reverend Gilbert, the minister at the Methodist church his aunt attended, had taken an interest in him. He was about as old as the oubaas, but he looked older, with a pale, drawn face and white hair and a worried look, always, in his kind eyes. He had been to university in South Africa and in England, and had tu-tored Tengo, particularly in science and math. History and English were easier to catch up in, but it had meant a lot of work, reading late into the night by the light of a tiny lamp the minister had given him, while the others in the house slept.

When the minister saw some of the clay animals Tengo had made, he suggested Tengo take art classes. But when Tengo realized how much effort would be needed to get through all of the subjects he required to pass the matriculation exam for college entrance he knew he would not be able to afford the time. Sometimes he would feel a yearning in his palms and fingertips for a lump of clay, and sometimes he would dream he was modeling clay figures. Yet, he wondered when he woke, if he were to work with clay now, what figures would he find concealed in the clay? What if, from out of his kneading, shaping, forming, something ugly emerged, something frightening?

He remembered the marble sculptures he had seen in the art book, and he thought, *Someday, when there is time, I will think of such things again . . . and perhaps . . .* But he wasn't able, or wouldn't allow himself, to complete the thought.

At first he had been put in a class with children younger than himself. But his determination to learn drove him, and he passed the tests easily and prepared for the examinations for entry into more advanced classes. Eventually he was able to write to his parents telling them that not only had he been placed in a class with students his own age, but he was now often at the top of the class.

His family longed to see him. The hut is empty without you, his mother wrote. But they understood that he could not take time away from his studies to come and see them. And a train ticket cost money. A visit home was a luxury they could not afford.

His cousins were always teasing him because they could not pull him away from his books to come out and play with them. But there was more pleasure for Tengo in his books than in kicking a soccer ball around in a dusty lot littered with old tires and rotting mattresses and foul-smelling heaps of refuse. There were many people without jobs—youths and men—who hung about on the streets empty-eyed, bored, dispirited. Even the trees—sparse among the sprawl of close-built, small, tin-roofed houses where a million people crowded—tall dusty palm-trees, sycamores, jacarandas here and there, had a defeated look.

It was not easy for Tengo to study. The four-room house was always full of people and clutter and noise. Relatives from other places often came to stay; visitors dropped in day and night; bare-bottomed babies crawled about, and small children ran in and out. His aunt and uncle both worked in the city and had to be up before it was light to catch the early train packed tight with bleary-eyed workers who spent so many hours traveling to their jobs that there was little time left for sleep. The grandmother took charge of the household during the day, but she was old and it was hard for her.

His aunt was a "tea-girl" in the office of an advertising agency in one of the tall skyscrapers in the city. "How can they call you a 'tea-girl,' Auntie," Joseph asked her once on one of his infrequent visits home, "when you are nearly fifty years old?"

She was harried and tired; she had just come in from work carrying a heavy bag of groceries; since by government decree there were no supermarkets or department stores in the township, she had to do all of her shopping in the city after work, lugging the bulging packages back home each night on overcrowded buses and trains. Before taking her coat off she put on a pot of water to start it boiling while she peeled the potatoes. "Oh, Joseph!" she said with exasperation, "the person who makes the tea for everyone in the office is always called the tea-girl. It's the name of the job, that's all."

The kitchen was small and cramped; there was no space for a dining table, and everyone ate in the living room with their plates on their laps while the television blared from its corner.

Tengo shared one of the bedrooms with his cousins. He trained himself to block out the noise and all the coming and going, concentrating his attention on his work. When exam time approached, he would go over to the church hall where the minister let him use a small back room to study in. His teachers encouraged him, and he knew they were proud of his success. They told him that if he continued the way he was going, he was sure to get a first-class matric which would help him gain a scholarship to go to college.

Whenever he came home, Joseph said little about what kept him away. Tengo was very fond of him and took time from his books whenever there was a chance to be with him. But he had changed—he had grown silent. He had dropped out of school just months before he was due to matriculate and go on to college. When Tengo asked why, he was reluctant to talk about it.

But one day, away from the tumult and the tightness of the house in the township, they had a talk. It was a Sunday. Joseph, home for a few days, invited Tengo to go into town with him to visit his mother who was unable to get off that weekend as the Millers were having a garden party. In the afternoon, since Matilda was busy, they took a walk to the Zoo Lake and sat down on the grass where people were picnicking under the trees or strolling beside the water or reading the Sunday papers. Dogs chased excitedly after thrown sticks or balls, and babies staggered about in the bright spring sunshine. There were brown ducks and a few rowboats out on the lake.

"It's nice here," Tengo said. He sprawled on the grass. "These days I hardly ever see anything green."

"When I was a child, blacks were not allowed to come and relax here at the Zoo Lake," Joseph said broodingly. "Now they allow us, and they think small things like this will satisfy us. They think they can quieten us by throwing a few crusts. . . ." He became silent, withdrawn.

When Joseph retreated this way into his anger, Tengo did not know how to reach him. He remained silent, watching the sky through the leaves.

Joseph felt in his pocket for a cigarette and lit up. Smoking seemed to relax him. He was a heavy smoker and had a chronic cough that his mother was always telling him was caused by cigarettes. "Dr. Miller has told you a dozen times that the cough won't go until you give up smoking," she would say as soon as his hand reached for his shirt pocket. But he was always tense and often jittery and seemed not to be able to do without them. "Leave me alone about the cigarettes, Ma," he would tell her. Now he stretched out on his back and blew the smoke up into the air. "At least it's nice and peaceful here away from the stink and noise of the township," he said.

Seeing him more at ease, Tengo asked, "Joseph, you always said you were going to matriculate and go to college. What happened?"

"Don't ask, Tengo. I don't want to put you off your studies."

"Tell me."

"What happened? Soweto happened."

"Soweto?"

"The first time all the schoolchildren went on strike. The first time they brought police into a township to fire on children and kill them just for protesting."

"What was the protest about?"

"The government wanted to make Afrikaans the official language in black schools. They wanted to force us to give up our English textbooks and do all our learning in their Boer language."

"But why?"

"Why? Because it's better for them if we remain ignorant and cut off by using a language no one else in the world can understand but the damned Afrikaners. This way they thought they could control us and keep us from having contact with the outside world. But they were wrong. Twenty thousand kids joined in the march. The police tried to stop them, and some of them began to throw stones. So the police opened fire, and killed a boy of thirteen. After that there was no stopping the children. They armed themselves with sticks and stones and dustbin lids against the gunfire, and the police kept on shooting until hundreds of people lay dead and thousands more were injured. It was war against unarmed school kids. So rioting and burning followed, and it spread to townships right across the country. The children didn't give in. And they won. They only went back to school when the plan for Afrikaans education was scrapped. I was still small, but I remember it well. After Soweto, young people began to feel their own power."

Tengo was quiet for a while, then he asked, "But then, why didn't you finish school, Joseph?"

"Because Soweto changed the outlook for many of us. After Soweto, I began to grow up; and I began to understand that instead of educating us, they are just throwing us a bone. In the black schools and universities, they're giving us an inferior education—gutter education. Bantu education is designed to make us better slaves."

As he listened to his cousin, Tengo felt a clutch of anxiety take hold of him. He didn't know if the teaching he was getting was inferior or not; he only knew that, for him, it opened doors that until then had remained shut and locked, that it satisfied his desire to know while at the same time it offered more and more to want to know about. For him it was like an endless feast. He remembered how it had been, all those years on the farm, with no way of looking for answers to the questions that came up whichever way he turned. It had felt like being tied down with rope when you wanted to run over the veld. No matter what Joseph said about it, for him it had more value than anything else.

Joseph sat up and ground out his cigarette in the grass. He looked down at Tengo who lay silently staring up into the blue of the sky. "What I am saying makes you worried, cousin?"

Tengo nodded his head.

"That is why I haven't wanted to talk to you of these things. You are still young. You have a lot to learn yet, especially because you've started school so late. Keep on with your studies, Tengo; I hear you are very smart. But I think that in time what is happening all around you will teach you—in its own way. And when the time comes, you will have to decide what is best for you."

"When the time comes? What time?" Tengo felt afraid.

Joseph stood up. "Come. That's enough serious talk for one day. Let's go back. Their party should be over by now. I'm sure there will be plenty of good food left over. If you are hungry, it is good to be around white liberals. They have trouble with their consciences, and it makes them generous."

"The Millers are white liberals?"

"That's right."

"Dr. Miller is paying for all my schoolbooks."

"Good. He can afford it," Joseph said shortly. "He

used to pay for mine too. It probably costs him much less than the fees for membership at his golf club."

Here was another way of looking at things. As they walked back through the quiet of Sunday in the suburbs, Tengo glanced at his cousin strolling beside him, hands in pockets, head lowered, whistling a silent tune. "Joseph," he asked him, "what do you do, where do you go when you're away from home?"

Not turning his head, Joseph said, "Better not to ask questions, cousin. The less you know, the less you can get in trouble."

CHAPTER

11

*F*or Frikkie the years at school dragged. When he was sixteen and had scraped through the junior certificate exam, he wanted to leave school, but his parents and uncle and aunt insisted he matriculate.

"Be sensible, old fellow," Oom Koos told him. "When you're eighteen you'll have to go into the army for two years anyway. So get your matric, do your military service, and when you're twenty, you'll come out and the farm will be waiting for you, and you'll become my assistant manager."

He went along with what they wanted; everything he had to do—passing exams, finishing school, going into the army—he regarded as something to be got out of the way so that he could begin his real life—on the farm.

Oom Koos taught him to drive the car, and he could take out the combine on his own; he liked tinkering with machines and became skilled at repairing mechanical parts when they broke down. Oom Koos talked of mechanizing the dairy. "Give me an efficient machine any day rather than a bunch of lazy kaffirs," he said. "Tell you what, Frikkie. When you come out of the army, we'll install milking machines. With a skilled mechanic like you on the farm it will make good sense."

Frikkie was shy with people his own age, but he became friendly with a girl—Ina, a classmate of Sissie's—and on Saturdays he would take her to the cinema and buy her a large block of chocolate which they would eat their way through, passing it to each other in the dark, their eyes fixed on the screen. Sissie teased Frikkie about Ina, but apart from talking about the film they had just seen, he never found much to say to her. As he walked her back to her house one night, he told her how he was going to become his uncle's farm manager, how they planned to mechanize the dairy.

"That's not the life for me," she said. "To be stuck out in the middle of nowhere. Nothing to look at but the boring veld. Nowhere to have a bit of fun. Not me!" She touched the curls behind her ear into place, and the charm bracelet on her wrist tinkled. "I'm going to learn shorthand and typing and get a secretarial job in television, or advertising, in Jo'burg. My cousin there goes to discos all the time. It's so dead here. If you don't go to the movies there's nothing to do but sit home and twiddle your thumbs. I can't wait to get out of here. You're lucky. You'll be in the army soon and away from this boring little dorp."

.   .   .

When he came home on his first leave from training camp, Ina was at the house with Sissie, and they both looked impressed by the sight of him in his khaki uniform with his buttons polished to a high shine, his big snub-toed boots gleaming, and his yellow hair cropped close to his skull. On Saturday night he took them both to the cinema, and they walked proudly, one on each side of him, along Main Street and through the cinema lobby crowded with their schoolmates. In the dark, Ina slipped her hand into his, making it difficult to break off squares of chocolate.

Though the army training was rigorous and demanding, Frikkie preferred it to school and found it pleasant to be an outstanding recruit after having been always a poor student. He did what was expected of him efficiently and conscientiously; his experience with the farm machinery stood him in good stead; he was strong and tireless on route marches and combat training; and his officers liked him. He got along with them better than he ever had with his schoolteachers. He enjoyed taking his rifle apart to clean it and oil it and fit the precision-engineered parts satisfyingly together again. He had been out hunting with Oom Koos for several seasons and was a crack shot.

He was stationed at a camp outside a small town not far from Johannesburg. He went into the city occasionally with some of his platoon mates, but he didn't care for the noise and the high buildings and the fast pace of life there. He made friends only with one boy, Pieter Uys, also a farm boy who longed to be back on his father's farm.

Tant Sannie sent on to him back copies of farming magazines, and in his spare time he would lie on his cot reading them and making plans for improving the farm when his army service was over. His captain suggested to him more than once that he should think about remaining in the force and becoming a professional soldier, promising him that he would soon become an officer. But after a time he gave up. "We're not going to be able to get this *plaas-seuntjie*—this farmer-boy—away from the land," he admitted at last.

When Frikkie had the chance of a few days off he headed for the farm. Oom Koos and Tant Sannie were proud to see their nephew in uniform.

"Army life is good for you, Frikkie," his aunt said. "Just look at the boy, Koos—he's almost as tall as you." She was knitting a khaki sweater for him; measuring the length of his arm for the sleeve, she prodded the brawny muscle of his upper arm. "Like iron," she said. "This country is safe in the hands of boys like you."

The farm workers gathered around in the yard to admire the kleinbaas in his uniform. "Hau, you're getting so big you're becoming the *groot-baas*—the big master," Timothy observed.

In the kitchen Selina stared at him. "My word! Kleinbaas Frikkie is a real soldier now."

"How's Tengo?" he asked. Since Tengo had gone, Frikkie had never been down to the kraal again.

"Oh, he's doing *so* well at school. He'll be writing matric this year. And they think he's going to be getting one of those scholarships to go to college. He writes to us that one day he wants to go and study in the *United States*! Can you imagine such a thing, Kleinbaas?"

"The United States!" Frikkie felt oddly put out at this;

but since he had acquired the habit throughout his unhappy days at school of dismissing from his mind the things that made him uneasy, he merely asked, "Any fruitcake, Selina?"

"Of course, Kleinbaas. As soon as the madam told me you would be here I straightaway baked one."

He went to his room to change out of his uniform, his heavy boots clumping loudly on the linoleum floor of the passage. The red clay bull was still on the chest of drawers, his soccer ball at the bottom of the wardrobe. He looked past the clay figure out of the window to where the long drought continued and the parched land baked, yellow and sere, under the sun; and he thought, *It was all so green when we were children.* Without touching it, he gazed at the little bull, which looked as if it had paused for an instant before breaking into a run, and he thought to himself, *United States. . . .*

At the tea table, over his third cup of tea and third slice of fruitcake, he said, "Selina says Tengo wants to go and study in the States."

Tant Sannie clicked her tongue.

"I'm telling you, Frikkie," Oom Koos said, grim lines around his mouth, "these blacks are really getting out of hand. All those liberals—those kaffir boeties overseas, who know nothing about the way agitators are stirring up the blacks in this country—they've given them ideas that make them believe they can become our equals. It's getting more and more difficult to keep them in their place. Now you have farm kaffirs wanting to go for education to the States—what next then?"

"What next is *they'll* be wanting to rule *us*," Tant Sannie put in.

"*Never.*" Oom Koos put down his teacup. "I would fight that with the last drop of my blood."

Tant Sannie patted her husband's arm. "Don't fret, Koos. With fine young men like Frikkie to defend us, the kaffirs will stay in their place." She gazed fondly at Frikkie.

"But they'll still make plenty of trouble for us," Frikkie said. "One of the units at our base was called out last week to help the police break up a demonstration in a township outside Pretoria. It was a dangerous mob. The police were seriously outnumbered, and our boys got there just in time to shoot a few of them and frighten the rest away. They were throwing petrol-bombs, rocks. . . ."

"The only language they understand is a strong arm." Oom Koos passed his cup along to be refilled. "It's all those children in the townships that are making the trouble. What good has education done them! It's only made them dissatisfied and greedy to take what is ours. If we give in to them on anything, they take it as a sign of weakness. You can't reason with the black mind. Force is the only way we're going to keep them under control."

"That's what our officers tell us in our training," Frikkie said.

"Things are bad enough in this country without all this trouble from the blacks," Oom Koos said. "This is the fourth year of the drought. If we don't get rain soon, I don't know, Frikkie. . . . I don't know how much of a farm will be waiting for you when you come out of the army."

Tant Sannie looked anxiously at her husband. "The rain will come, Koos, the rain will come. Be patient—the Lord will answer our prayers." She touched his huge, thick-fingered hand and spoke soothingly as if he were a baby. "The rain will come." She sugared and stirred his tea and set it down in front of him. "Drink your tea now, Koos, and stop worrying. The doctor has told you that worrying is bad for your blood pressure."

They finished their tea in silence. When Selina came in to clear the table, Tant Sannie said, "Wrap up the rest of the cake, Selina. The kleinbaas can take it back to camp with him."

"I wish we had you cooking for us at camp, Selina," Frikkie said. "The food there is awful."

"Hau, poor Kleinbaas." Selina looked at him with sympathy. "You'd better eat as much as you can while you're with us."

Back at the army base, Frikkie marked time; he marched; drilled in the unrelenting sun; ran for miles; plodded on route marches; did target practice, learned to use tear gas, rubber bullets, hand grenades, machine guns; went to lectures about terrorism, about urban guerilla warfare, about black liberation groups; polished his buttons and buckles and boots; and made up his bed each morning square and tight to pass inspection by the sergeant, compared with whom Snake Steenkamp seemed a meek, mild-mannered man. Whatever he was doing, he was waiting—waiting to get out of his stiff uniform into soft, worn work clothes; waiting until every day he could feel the glossy warmth of a cow's flank under his palm; until from his seat high up on the tractor he could look behind him and see the red earth curling over to fall into straight regular ridges and furrows under the blades of the plow; until he could smell the sunshiny dust in the threshing chamber and the summer sweetness stored in the hay bales piled to the roof in the storage shed. Each night he fell asleep on his narrow army cot picturing the time when he would wake up in the mornings to the sound of the rooster crowing in the first light as the fresh new day whitened the sky outside the windows of his room at the farm.

CHAPTER

12

*T*engo didn't recognize the flowers in the bed he was weeding; none of them had bloomed in the garden at the farm. When he was a piccanin he used to weed for the wife of the oubaas, but her beds were planted with only two or three kinds of flowers. The Millers' garden looked like a picture in a book. Mrs. Miller knew all about gardening. She told him what should be planted in the shade and what needed full sun and where old plantings should be thinned and divided and how shrubs should be pruned. She would come out every morning wearing a big sun hat and explain to Tengo what had to be done.

He had mowed the lawns. They looked like smooth green carpets spread out between the swimming pool and the tennis court.

After the years of sitting hunched over books studying by poor light, it felt good to get his fingers in the damp earth again, with the sun on his back and the birds chirping in the treetops. Lucky, Tengo thought, that it was during the school holidays that the Millers' gardener had been called home to his sick wife. After the long absence from the farm, it was pleasure for him to have a chance to work in the garden for a month, and to be earning good money as well.

Reverend Gilbert had encouraged him to take the job when his auntie had told him the Millers were looking for a temporary gardener. "You've worked hard all these years, Tengo," he'd said. "You've overdone it, I think. You've never taken time off from your studying. Give yourself a break. Physical work will do you good after the mental effort you've expended. And after the holidays, just one more year to go. I'm confident you'll get a first-class matric, my lad. So just forget about the books for a month, enjoy the good weather, and take things easy."

The Miller children were on holiday from school as well. There were only three of them now. The two older boys had left the country rather than do their military service. They were both studying overseas and could never come back to South Africa again, his auntie had told him; if they did, they would be either drafted into the army or arrested. Dr. and Mrs. Miller went every year now, first to England to visit one son, then to the States to see the other.

It was quiet and peaceful here in the northern suburbs. It was hard to believe that the din and dirt of the township was not many miles away; it seemed like another world. Having the gardener's room all to himself was a rare experience, and there was plenty to eat. In the warm, drowsy afternoon, doves cooed in the roof over the garage, and insects hummed in the grass. The soothing sounds took Tengo back to summer days on the farm.

There had been a letter from his mother just before the school term ended.

Tandi is back from the hospital. It seems the treatment they gave her is working. She coughs very little now, but she is very thin. She must go back to the doctor for injections for quite a time yet. He says that she has T.B. Your granny and your father are in good health. Kleinbaas Frikkie was here for a visit. He looks a real soldier in his uniform. We went to see your cousin Benjamin at Meneer Van Rensburg's farm on Sunday. He is home for the holidays. He told us that there is a lot of trouble in the schools in the township. Now your father and I are worrying about you. We want you to be very careful, my son. Keep out of trouble. The most important thing for you now is to pass your matric and go to college. Do not let other things get in your way, no matter what others tell you. If you want a better life, education and a good job are what matters. . . .

Tengo pulled at a deep-rooted weed and it came up with a satisfying wrenching sound. He shook the clumped soil off the roots and sat back, squatting on his heels. *Do not let other things get in your way no matter what others tell you,* his mother wrote. If she only knew, he thought, how many things were getting in his way— so many that it was a wonder he had managed to write his exams at all. The rallying cry of the squads of militant students sounded in his ears chanting in unison:

Liberation first—education after!
Liberation first—education after!

He tried not to listen to them when they urged him to boycott classes. He closed his mind to what they were saying. He was set on a course that he couldn't allow anything to steer him away from. He knew what they said was true—that the education they got in black schools was inferior, that the government had decided long ago that there was no need to educate blacks beyond the level they would need for menial work, that most of their teachers hadn't completed high school themselves, and that in white classrooms there were fewer than twenty students to a teacher, while in his school there were over forty.

The militant students wanted to boycott classes until conditions for blacks were changed. But while Tengo agreed with them about how unjust and unfair it all was, he didn't want to look up from his books until he achieved what he had set out to do, what he had left the farm for.

"I can't think about things like revolution now," he told his friend Elijah, who was an activist. "I have too much work to do, man. When I have got my university degree, then I'll be able to put my mind to those things."

"The time for action is now, man, Tengo," Elijah said. "Everything is heating up. Soon it will be dangerous to try to go to school. The youth squads will start to enforce a school boycott. There's even talk of preventing our parents from going to work until the system starts to give in to our demands."

Tengo felt his stomach tighten with anxiety. "I can't talk to you now, Elijah. It's too close to examination time. I must go home now and study." He had walked home thinking about Elijah's cousin, who had won a scholarship to study in an American college.

. . .

His auntie came around the side of the house and called across the lawn. "Tengo, it's teatime. Your tea's on the table in the yard."

He sat under the jacaranda tree sipping sweet hot tea from a large enamel mug, and a picture rose up in his mind—Frikkie and himself under the jacaranda in the yard at the farm, the mauve blossoms carpeting the ground. He rarely thought of Frikkie. When he did, it was always with a feeling that disturbed him, and he would dismiss him quickly from his thoughts. He recalled now how he had once made a span of clay oxen and set them in two rows under a small wooden yoke; they looked as if they were patiently pulling a heavy load. Then Tandi had accidentally broken one of them and the whole thing was spoiled; the yoke collapsed and the oxen fell over. That was the feeling, he thought as he drank his tea, that he experienced when he thought of Frikkie—something spoiled, by accident . . . but what accident?

Claire came out of the house. She was a university student now, at the big white university in Johannesburg. She was carrying some books and came and sat down on the bench beside him. "Tengo, I'm sorting out all the books I don't need. These are art books and art history. Could you use them?"

"I don't think so. Thank you. I haven't got time for anything like that. I have too much studying to do for my matric." The books lay on the table, and he averted his eyes from them. He didn't even want to look at the titles—not now.

"Do you still do those clay sculptures?" she asked.

"No."

"What a pity. I thought you had a real talent. I draw. I had an idea of becoming an artist. But I decided to do architecture instead. I can be of more use to society as an architect."

"You want to design houses? Blocks of flats?"

"Oh no! Nothing like that. I'm interested in community design—planned urban projects."

"What sort?"

"Well . . . My dream is, one day, when this terrible government is thrown out, and the country is being decently run—*one person, one vote*—decent housing and schooling and health care for everyone—my dream is to design ideal community projects—townships with good houses and gardens for everyone, clinics, schools, day-care centers, recreation centers for old people, parks, swimming pools, sports stadiums. . . ."

While she spoke, Tengo pictured what she described, as if it were appearing on a television screen behind his eyes, transforming the township. "You could design all this?" he asked.

"Why not? That's going to be the subject of my final year project—an ideal planned community to replace an existing township. How about you, Tengo? What plans are you making?"

"I have one more year to go. Then I write matric. I'd like to go to college in the Cape. I've never been out of the Transvaal. I'd like to see the sea one day."

"What will you study?"

"I'm not sure yet. There's too much still that I want to know, that I have to learn, before I find out what I want to do."

She got up to go indoors. "Here, have this book, Tengo.

It's a history of art. It's very good. Keep it to read after matric."

At the end of the holidays, when it was time to go back to the township for the beginning of the school year, Dr. Miller paid Tengo generously.

Tengo thanked him. He no longer clasped his palms together before accepting something, as he had done in the old days. And he no longer called white people master or madam. His cousin Joseph had told him it was a mark of servitude to address whites this way.

"It's been good having you with us, Tengo," Dr. Miller said. They shook hands. "It looks as if it's been a wise investment, helping you through school. Matilda tells me your teachers are expecting you to get a first-class matric."

"I hope so," Tengo said.

"I'll be happy to go on helping you when you're at college, Tengo."

"Thank you," Tengo said.

When Tengo got back to the township, Joseph was at the house.

"Your mother didn't tell me you were here," Tengo said, happy to see him.

"She doesn't know. I'm only here overnight. I leave again early tomorrow morning."

Tengo knew now not to ask Joseph where he had been, where he was going, what the purpose of his visit was. He knew that if he really wanted to know, Joseph would tell him. And once he was told, it would be like having

to carry an extra burden; there would have to be deci-
sions made, and choices, once he shouldered the weight
of what Joseph was involved in. And right now Tengo
felt in no position to take on anything that disturbed the
course he was set on. So he asked no questions. And
Joseph told him nothing.

After supper the two of them sat outside on plastic
garden chairs in the small concrete forecourt of the
house. The sunset flared in deep red splendour over the
bleak expanse of the township. Joseph lit a cigarette.
"Who's this Emma I have been hearing about?" he
teased.

"Oh, she's just a girl in my class," Tengo said casually.
"She and I always compete for first place."

"Who wins?"

"Sometimes she does. Sometimes I do. She's also going
on to college. She's been spending the holidays at her
grandmother's kraal."

The tip of Joseph's cigarette glowed in the dusk. Tengo
described to him now the picture Claire had drawn of
the ideal planned community that she would design to
replace the dismal slum around them. Joseph listened as
Tengo spoke, his cigarette burning low till it scorched his
fingers. He swore and ground it out, then reached into his
pocket and lit up another.

"You think that sounds wonderful, do you, Tengo?"

"Of course. Look at all this—" He pointed to the vista
of small brick houses packed tight under peaked tin roofs
—grim, mean, the pall of smog reddened by the sinking
sun. "This is no way for human beings to live."

"It's an efficient way to house your black labour force—
at a distance far enough away so that you don't have to
smell the stink of their poverty, and close enough to town

so that they can get to your factories and offices in time to keep your economy rolling and your luxurious way of life taken care of."

"But Joseph, that's what she's against too!"

"Oh Tengo, Tengo, can't you see? Those white liberals, their hearts are in the right place, but they have no real understanding of what's at stake now. It's *too late*—too late for their goodwill, for their enlightened self-interest. They've got so much to lose. For us, there is only gain."

"But Joseph, she talked about these plans all happening *after* this government has been got rid of. She talked about *one-person-one-vote*."

"Of course. Listen, cousin. White liberals—I'm not saying they're not good people. Without them this place would be unrelieved hell. But they only alleviate the misery; they don't *change* things. They have consciences; it makes them uneasy to see unfairness, poverty, suffering. They don't *like* to see people thrown in jail for protesting, or small black kids suffering from malnutrition. It makes them uncomfortable. They can't enjoy their luxury while this is going on around them."

"But that's better—isn't it?—than people who *don't* feel uncomfortable. Better than people who think this is the way it's *supposed* to be for blacks?"

"Sure." Joseph pulled deeply on his cigarette, exhaling a sigh with the smoke. "And there *are* whites who are working with us for real change—people who are prepared to make sacrifices and put themselves in danger and go to jail, who understand that the blacks have to be *free*, not just uplifted to a more decent level. But people like Claire—you see, what they imagine is a future where we are all living happily in our ideally planned townships while *they* are all still living in their beautiful houses in the suburbs with their swimming pools full of filtered water and their tennis courts rolled and marked out with neat white lines." He fiercely stubbed out his half-smoked cigarette. "Well, I've got news for all those nice people. *It's too late now*. They've had their chance, and they've missed it! When *we* take over this country, *if* they're lucky, if they're still *alive*, *they* can live in their nice architect-planned townships! Our people will be living in those beautiful houses, and *our* children will be swimming in those swimming pools instead of running about hungry and ignorant in places like this!" Joseph was leaning forward as he spoke, his nostrils flaring and his fingers urgently gripping his knees.

Tengo drew in his breath sharply, shocked at his cousin's words and the vehemence that had built up and spilled over Claire's ideal of the future.

"We'll take over their houses," Joseph went on, "and we'll use them for official residences and for clubs and schools and clinics—for the *public* good! We'll give them to people with big families. Look how many of us are packed into this . . . this hovel"—he pointed bitterly at the house behind them—"while those Millers—five of them plus three servants—have a huge mansion to themselves!"

"But Joseph," Tengo persisted, "I understand what you say, but all the same those Millers are good people. There are not so many like them among the whites."

"I know, I know, Tengo. But they want to help us without giving up what they've got. And if it's going to be *fair shares*, there isn't enough to go round. There are twenty-two million of us and only four and a half million of them. And it's too late now. Man, can't you see? There's been too much suffering among our people. Too much pain. Too much bitterness. And now it's all built up into terrible anger, Tengo. *More terrible than they can imagine*. And out of this anger the change is going to come. It can't be stopped now. This Boer government, they can sense our power. They're frightened at last. They think they can stop the flood now with a few concessions—like abolishing the Pass Laws. But we *still* have to carry identity documents; and even if there are no more Pass Laws now to stop us from coming into the towns, it makes no difference. There are no jobs for us there and no place for us to live. They throw us a few crumbs. But it's too little, cousin, and too late. It can't be stopped now. And the goodwill of the liberal whites will be swept away with all the bad things we have to get rid of. I don't know if it can survive what's coming."

They were both silent. The sun had gone down, leaving only a pale glow of yellow in the darkening sky, as if from a distant bonfire. Tengo, recognizing the truth of his cousin's words, was afraid, feeling there was no one to turn to for certainty, for security. The grown-ups are no longer in charge, he thought; white and black, they have been unable to protect us—and now something was coming, was already on its way. And it frightened him that young people should have the power to bring it about.

"It's a pity, then. . . ." Tengo said.

"Yes. A lot of things are a pity."

He had trodden on ground he had been avoiding. It was as if he had unexpectedly stepped on a concealed explosive device when he had spoken to Joseph about Claire's design.

It was hard for him to fall asleep that night. He lay in the dark, listening in the small house to the sounds of its sleeping occupants—the steady breathing, sudden sighs, murmurs, snoring, a baby whimpering and being quieted by its mother on the couch in the living room where they were both spending the night. He had tried hard, since he'd left the farm, to narrow his sights, to keep single-mindedly to his studies, his need to find answers to the welter of questions the world presented him. The more he learned, he found, the more there was to know; the answers presented new sets of questions. There was nothing that gave him the same deep satisfaction that he got from his studies—looking up facts in books, fitting them in with what he already knew, working them into the essays he wrote, solving equations . . . bringing some shape and order to the press of existence he had felt on him even as a small child watching the days and seasons as they turned and unfolded over the unknown vastness of the veld. Except for modeling in clay, he admitted to himself in the close darkness that was alive with other people's dreaming—sculpting, Claire called it. But that was something to be put off for a later time, a time when. . . . His imagination left off there, as it always did.

More and more, it seemed now, the hidden land mines were cropping up everywhere underfoot; he never knew when or where another would go off, no matter how he tried to protect himself from the knowledge that history had sown them, over the years, and they could explode in any place at any time. Joseph was driven by his bitterness to try to bring about change; and though he had never said as much to him, Tengo knew that if change could come only through violence, then Joseph supported violence. He knew that Joseph was right not to accept the way things were for the blacks. He had learned that in no other place in the world were people deprived of human rights just because of the color of their skin. In some way, he had always known all this—from childhood, really, watching the oubaas and his wife, the way they treated his mother and father, the way Frikkie took for granted that the land and all of its privileges were for him because he was white, and that someone like himself must just accept what was thrown to him because he was black. He had never been able to accept that this was how it must be, the way his parents and his grandmother and his aunts and uncles seemed to accept it.

But he was afraid now. . . . Listening to Joseph this evening, feeling the thrust of his rage, made Tengo fear the destructiveness of the force that would have to be let loose for the change to be brought about. In the narrow iron cot next to his, Joseph muttered in his sleep, then cried out hoarsely, turned over, and was still again. Staring into the darkness Tengo felt a great surge of sorrow—for himself, for Joseph, for all of them taking refuge in sleep in the small crowded house—that they were living in a time and a place that would not allow them to lead peaceful lives in peaceful ways.

Very early in the morning, before it was light, he heard Joseph get out of bed and dress in the dark. He heard the front door as it was quietly opened and then closed again. Straining his ears, he heard the gate squeak, and then silence.

CHAPTER

13

T he new school year opened, and Tengo put all thought of unrest and revolution out of his mind. Reverend Gilbert had told him that if the final examinations went well there was an assured college scholarship for him from a synagogue in Johannesburg. He concentrated on his schoolwork, keeping out of the political discussion that simmered like a stew in a pot over a fire kept constantly fueled; among his schoolmates and in the crowded living room at home, the talk was about informers whose homes were burned to the ground, of schoolchildren being beaten and shot and arrested at protest demonstrations all over the country. Police and soldiers in their menacing armored trucks were becoming a familiar sight in the township, and some days on his way to and from school Tengo passed burning cars or mounds of tires set alight by angered mobs or placed as barricades against the clubs and guns of the police.

From time to time classmates would not appear in the mornings at their desks, and the word would go out that they had been arrested at a protest gathering or merely pulled out of their beds in the dark of night and taken away, suspected of being student leaders. Occasionally, someone would just disappear, and there would be whispers that he had "gone across the border." Amid the mounting anger and the fear of the ruthlessness of the authorities, Tengo kept to himself, studying with an almost desperate urgency. He felt like a hungry person at a laden table hurriedly eating his fill because someone was coming to pull the cloth out from under; food and dishes would crash to the ground, and there was no knowing where the next meal would come from.

During the day, at lunch break, or in the evenings, at dinner, he would keep a book handy—one of his English textbooks—and would concentrate on Dickens or Shakespeare while around him the ferment of argument and discussion continued about the growing disorder and unrest that were spreading faster than the authorities could contain them. Though the government forbade journalists and television crews from reporting the violent clashes between protestors and the police and army, the news spread like a flame running along a fuse wire.

Trouble was in the air and on the streets and part of everyone's conversation, along with the smell of scorched rubber that hung in a pall over the township from the piles of burning tires. But Tengo kept his sights fixed firmly on the final examinations and his scholarship, and remained apart from the turmoil around him.

"Tengo," his friend Elijah warned him, "if you don't join us soon, the comrades are going to start thinking that perhaps you are being paid to work for our enemies."

A chill of fear stirred Tengo's heart. "Come on, man, Elijah," he said. "You know which side I'm on. I just

need some time, man. I started school so much later
than all of you. I have to work much harder to catch up.
After matric, man, after matric . . . I can't afford time
to do anything but study now. Ask them to leave me
alone until then."

Elijah laughed and punched Tengo lightly on the arm.
"Don't worry, brother. We know you're all right. Your
cousin Joseph vouches for you. Keep on with your studies,
my friend. We'll make you minister for culture when
the day comes and we're running this country."

The days cooled off a little as autumn came on. Tengo
woke one morning, looked at the clock, and saw he had
overslept. He dressed hurriedly, washed at the cold tap in
the yard, gulped down his tea and bread. Though he
didn't like being late for school, he was in a good mood.
He had sat up very late the night before, finishing an
essay, and he was pleased with the way it had turned out.
Its subject was the cause and effects of the Great Trek,
and he had picked out as his theme the Afrikaners' own
view of themselves as bearers of the Covenant, as if it
was their God-given mission to sustain white supremacy
in South Africa, finding their justification for maintain-
ing blacks always as menials by regarding them as the
children of Ham who were to remain "hewers of wood
and drawers of water."

He was sure his history teacher would give him a
high mark for the essay. He would show it to Reverend
Gilbert, too, he decided, as he walked quickly to school.
He wanted to talk with the minister about the way the
Boers turned the Bible to their own cruel purpose.

Reflecting on the way he had written his argument and
his conclusion that the Afrikaners' narrow, zealous way

of seeing would lead them to their own destruction, he
neared school before he grew aware something was going
on.

The police trucks known as "hippos" roaming the
township had become so much a part of everyday reality
that Tengo no longer took much notice of them. But today
there was the deafening chatter of helicopters above the
rooftops, and in the vicinity of the school a number of
military armored trucks—Casspirs, designed for bush
warfare—were making their way along the dusty, pot-
holed streets. Surrounding the school yard, at five-yard
intervals from each other, soldiers with rifles stood at
attention.

Schoolchildren were milling and shouting inside the
school yard, many of them calling taunts through the
fence at the soldiers. Across the street a unit of the youth
squad, in their khaki shorts and shirts and black berets,
their pockets bulging with stones, were trying to prevent
students from going toward the school gates. Other students, carrying placards, were marching up and down
the road, chanting: "Liberation first! Education after!"

Tengo felt a sickening lurch in his chest. He saw Alice,
Elijah's sister, holding up a placard with the words "Stop
the Killing of School Children." He went up to her.
"What's happening, Alice?"

"We're boycotting classes today. We're commemorat-
ing the death of Betty Mikwena. It's a year today that she
was run over by a police truck in the middle of a peaceful demonstration. *Don't go into school today, Tengo*—no
matter what! It will look bad for you if you do. *I'm
warning you.*" In a low voice, close to Tengo's ear, she
muttered, "The comrades are going to think you're a
police stooge." Then she raised her placard and hurried
off to catch up with her group.

Suddenly there were two blue-uniformed riot police-men, one on each side of Tengo. "Are you on your way to school, kaffir?" one asked in Afrikaans. Before he could answer, they each grabbed him by an arm and frog-marched him across the street; then, with a rough push, they shoved him through the gate so that he fell and found himself sprawling on the ground with his school-bag burst open and his books and papers scattered around him. His neatly written essay with its narrow margin and the title underlined in red ballpoint, lay on the dusty ground, its pages fluttering and separating in the breezy morning.

Tengo felt a rush of terrible rage shake him. He got up and gathered the pages before they could blow away, picked up his books, and repacked his bag. Then he turned and started to walk out through the gate. A soldier at the gate pointed his rifle at him. "You have to stay in the school," he said. "It is not permitted to leave."

In his anger he felt he would rather be shot by the weapon pointed at him than submit to the white uni-formed men forming a chain around the school. Un-heeding, he pushed forward.

"Stay where you are!" the soldier shouted. At that moment a hail of stones came pelting through the air from across the road. The soldiers at the gate and the two policemen whipped around, and Tengo slipped quickly through and merged with a crowd that had surged up on the pavement. A group of policemen jumped down from a truck, flailing their sticks through the crowd. Tengo heard the sound of their batons on skulls and backs. There were screams. He pushed past a girl with blood streaming down her forehead, and made his way out of the press of people and across the road.

Alice came running up to him. "Good work, Tengo! We started throwing stones to help you. Come and join us now, comrade. Marcus has been hurt. You can take over his placard."

But Tengo pushed past her, blind almost, and deaf to everything but the force of the paroxysm of hate that stormed in him. He pushed on through the township, carried by the fury that had erupted when he had found himself sprawling on the ground with the pages of his essay fluttering senselessly about like garbage blown by the wind. His mouth was dry, one side of his head splitting with pain, and there was a roaring in his ears.

He went straight back to the house. No one was home. Everyone had gone to work. Even the old grandmother went into the city three days a week now, to do washing and ironing. The continuing unrest all over the country was having a bad effect on business, many people were without jobs, and the cost of food had gone up. The extra money the old lady earned, Tengo knew, meant more money for food for all of them. He knew, too, that with no adults in the house, his young cousins were running wild and using the disorder as an excuse to shirk their schoolwork. He had passed them on his way home, smoking and laughing with a group of boys and girls near the church hall.

In the bedroom he sat down at the rickety table he used as his desk. Elbows on the table, he covered his eyes with his hands. In the dark behind his eyelids he saw himself, over and over again, pushed and hurled sprawling to the ground, the contents of his schoolbag lying worthless in the dust. In his ears, the voices of the police, the soldier's shouted command, repeated again and again. He felt something he desperately wanted slipping away from him, felt powerless to hold onto it. His rage turned into loss, to grief, and great dry sobs shook his chest. In the silence of the small house he could hear his own weeping. Overhead, above the roof of the house, the chopping sound of a passing helicopter set the dishes and ornaments and picture frames rattling.

Another time, a different event—but not so different— had shaken him this way, he recalled. Years ago, at the farm, when a young white girl had ordered old Ezekiel to obey her command and had spoken to him as if he were one of the mongrel farm dogs—that was the first time he had experienced this bitter resentment. No, it had been earlier, when the madam had ordered him out of the bedroom of that pink-faced little Sissie. It had stunned him, baffled him then. But this time, fired up by the brutality of the police and the soldiers, it had a force and a fury that frightened him. Gripped, possessed by it, he felt afraid of what he might be capable of if he found himself provoked by them again. He knew that even if the hurled stones had not diverted the soldier he would have made his way out through the school gate no matter what the consequences might have been.

Against his cheek his hand felt sticky and warm. He looked and saw a red bloody abrasion across the heel of his left hand where it had broken his fall. His left hip ached where it had hit the ground. The left knee of his new jeans was torn. He had bought them with some of the money he had earned working for the Millers; the rest he had sent home to his parents.

He groaned. *How am I going to go on now*, he wondered. *What has happened today is a terrible thing. . . .* How was he going to be able to put all of this aside now, to get on with his studies, his first-class matric? What if his rage caught fire now, every time he saw a policeman, a soldier?

What he was always afraid to look at, to listen to, to acknowledge in Joseph was burning now inside himself. Again, he groaned out loud. Whom could he turn to? His parents lived in another world; they couldn't help him, couldn't even understand. Joseph? Elijah? They would pull him into the very belly of what he had been trying to avoid, to postpone. Reverend Gilbert? He was kind, wise, filled with compassion—but he was white. With all his deep human sympathy, it was not possible for him truly to understand what it meant to Tengo— his experience today at the hands of the white uniformed men. With all of his commitment to the suffering of the blacks, the minister looked out at the world from inside a white skin.

Tengo felt himself faltering on the edge of a pit, with everything he had worked for, everything he valued, scattered useless behind him and only the unknown darkness ahead. He laid his head down on his arms on the desk, not weeping anymore, filled with despair.

For the rest of the week there was no school. The authorities put locks and chains on the gates, police patrolled the fence, and there was an announcement that the school would remain closed while the "unruly element" was rounded up so that it would be safe for "decent, law-abiding" students to attend classes without harassment.

At three in the morning the police raided houses where they believed leaders of the student uprising lived, and Elijah and his sister Alice were among the many young people rounded up and arrested. A parents' committee was formed to demand the release of their children and to make depositions about beating and ill-treatment of the children while they were being held in jail.

Through all this, Tengo remained indoors and solitary. From the talk of his cousins and the others in the house, he knew what was going on, but he kept to himself, his spirit low, his enthusiasm for his studies gone. His essay, in which he had taken so much pride, seemed meaningless now; it remained on his desk, its neatly written lined pages creased and smudged with dirt. He lay on his bed most of the day, reading dog-eared paperbacks he found around the house, stories of the Wild West and thrillers about gangsters in Chicago and New York.

"You're not eating your food, Tengo," his aunt chided him. "Are you not feeling well?"

"I'm all right, Auntie. I'm not hungry."

She looked anxiously at him. "Until the school opens again, my boy, why don't you go and ask Reverend Gilbert to coach you with your lessons? Ask him to give you homework. Your cousins are enjoying being out of school, I'm sorry to see. But you've got your matric coming up. Go see the reverend, Tengo."

"Maybe I will, Auntie." But he felt listless and made no effort to do what his aunt suggested.

In the middle of the second week of the school closing, there was a knock at the door one afternoon as Tengo lounged on the sofa watching a television program for young children. The door was open, and Reverend Gilbert came in.

Embarrassed, Tengo scrambled to his feet and turned off the television. "Good afternoon, Reverend. Come in. Sit down. Can I get you something to drink? Tea?"

"A glass of water will be fine, thank you, Tengo." He ran his finger under his stiff white clerical collar. "It's a hot day to be dressed in black serge."

He sat down in a worn leather armchair that had come

from Dr. Miller's study, drank the water, then looked at Tengo opposite him on the sofa. "Missing school, my lad?"

Tengo nodded.

"I thought you must be feeling bored. I've brought you some books to read." He reached into the canvas satchel that was slung always from his shoulder as he went about the township. From it he would take sweets or biscuits or small toys for children, official forms he had obtained for parishioners, vitamin C tablets he would press on anyone who had a cold, stamps, adhesive tape. . . . The minister's army-surplus satchel was a source of gentle joking in the township. "Here they are. They're not part of the matric syllabus, Tengo. But they'll enrich these days of enforced idleness for you. Here—this one is three short novels of Joseph Conrad. I hope you'll like *The Shadow Line* as much as I do. Try this Camus, *The Stranger*. It has great power. And here is a collection of stories by Chekov."

"Thank you, Reverend." Tengo took the books.

"There's a rumor the schools will be opening next week."

Tengo remained silent.

"You must be keen to get back."

"Reverend Gilbert," Tengo blurted out. "I'm very worried. If school opens next week, this isn't the end of it. It's only the beginning. It's going to be happening again and again—what happened last week. I'm frightened now that they're—that it's going to become impossible for me to write my matric."

"Don't say that, my lad! Don't even think it! Even if things become upset and disrupted, you can stick to the course. You know the syllabus. Your teachers can give

you work that you can do on your own. And I can coach
you. You can come to me. I'll give you all the help you
need. Okay, Tengo?" he asked as the boy made no reply.
"Will you do that?"

"That's only part of what's worrying me," he said,
looking down at the square of worn carpet on the
scrubbed linoleum floor. "You see . . . they're going to
start putting pressure on me—the comrades—to boycott
classes." He looked up at the minister. "It's very hard,
Reverend. You see, I agree with them. What they're
doing is *right*. I know we have to take our freedom ourselves. *They're never going to give it to us*," he said with
sudden bitterness. "Myself, I don't like violence. But
how else can we deal with *their* violence?" He turned
the palms of his hands up in a gesture of helplessness.
"So I *know*—even though I don't want to, I know I'm
going to have to join the struggle. But all along I have
been hoping . . . that I could just . . . first finish my
matric, you see. . . ."

As he listened to Tengo, the minister's face set in an
expression of deep sadness. He came over and sat on the
sofa and put his arm around the boy's shoulders. "Oh
Tengo, my boy, my boy . . ." he said. He looked out the
window at the clear blue sky that blazed over the desolation of the township.

In the silence Tengo thought, *He is searching for the
words that will comfort me. But there are none. . . .*

"Oh Tengo, it's hard for you. I know how hard it is.
What a terrible wrong it is that a boy like you should
find himself trapped this way. A terrible wrong . . . I
have to pray to God to give me the strength not to lose
hope in the face of what this government is doing to
black people—to children. I don't like the violence and

the tactics of the comrades. But they have been *forced* into existence by the cruelty, the injustice. And they have no other choice but to oppose it—to meet violence with violence. I say this—and I call myself a man of peace. So much suffering already . . . and so much more still to come, before the wrongs are set right."

"The ones who are really in the struggle, like Elijah and Alice, they are blaming our parents. They say our parents should not have put up with all this, with what the system does to the black people."

The minister shook his head sadly. "Don't go blaming your parents. They've suffered. They've always wanted things better for their children. They didn't really understand the nature—the intransigence—of white power. But your generation has the advantage of history, Tengo —the end of the colonial period, independent black African states, the civil rights movement in America, black consciousness. . . . Your generation has been born into a different time, with different possibilities. And now, the terrible burden of changing it all falls to you."

"I know I have to become part of it, Reverend, part of the struggle. But my parents—they've sacrificed a lot to put me through school. I could have been working and earning, instead of costing them money to support me. They have borrowed money from the oubaas at the farm, and he takes it off their wages every month."

The minister gripped his shoulder. "Tengo. You've come this far. Don't let it spill—and waste. Stay with it. If classes are disrupted, work on your own. Come to me. I'll help you all I can. Sit your matric. There are plenty of freedom fighters. There are not that many Tengos. When South Africa is free one day, they'll *need* people like you. Stay with what you've started, Tengo, and finish it."

Tengo was quiet, thinking over the minister's words. "But what if they say," he asked then, "what if they say to me, you sat over your books instead of fighting beside us, so you're not entitled to be part of our society in the new Azania?"

"I pray to God that they won't be so foolish and short-sighted not to realize that their educated people will be a rich resource in their new society, no less valuable than uranium and gold."

"What if they call me traitor?"

The minister sighed. He reached over and scrabbled in his satchel and took out a pipe and tobacco pouch. "Mind if I smoke?"

Tengo shook his head.

Reverend Gilbert filled the pipe bowl, struck a few matches until it lit up, exhaled, and the house filled with the fragrance of his tobacco. He puffed in silence for a while, then said, "It won't be easy for you, Tengo. You have to decide—is it worth it? They'll put a lot of pressure on you. Neither of the choices is an easy one." His pipe was not drawing well. Tamping it and relighting it, to himself he wondered: Why, dear Lord, why is it ordered so that the right choice is always the hard one? Can there never be a choice that is easy, and right? How I would love to get this boy out of here, send him elsewhere, to save him. But would he be saved then? "It's going to be hard whatever you do—joining them or sticking with your studies," he said, brushing ash off his trouser legs. "Whichever you settle on will take a lot of courage. There is no easy way. I would like to see you continuing your education."

"It will be hard, Reverend," Tengo said.

The minister stood up. "I'll pray for you, Tengo. I have great faith in you."

He looked at Tengo, his kind brown eyes filled with sadness, his smile pained. Tengo thought, *I should be comforting him because there is so little he can do. . . .*

The minister fastened the straps of his satchel, slung it over his shoulder, and took his leave. At the gate he knocked his pipe out against the fence post and slipped it into his pocket.

"Thank you for the books, Reverend," Tengo called from the doorway.

The minister waved. "Read them," he said. He patted the heads of two small children playing in the dust. "Mind, out of my way," the larger child was yelling at his playmate, "I am coming in the hippo to shoot you down." The other, no more than four years old, the reverend thought, pointed a finger and took aim at his companion. "Bang! Bang! I've killed you. I've killed all the Boers! You're dead." Reverend Gilbert went on his way, his shoulders bowed, a frown creasing his forehead and scoring his cheeks.

C H A P T E R
14

*T*engo tried reading the books the minister had lent him, but even stories and novels, in which there was always pleasure and escape for him, could not hold his attention; he found himself looking at words that refused to connect and went their own way—like wayward oxen that could not be brought together under one yoke. He leafed from one story to the next in the hope that his interest would be pulled in by a character or a plot, but he ended up gazing listlessly out of the window. He felt as if something that he had depended on for support had been knocked out of his grasp, and he drifted, unsteady, unsure.

After three weeks the schools opened again. The return to classes and routines and schedules of lessons and homework gave him something to cling to once more, and he studied with renewed intensity. The matriculation exam became the reality he depended on; he was sure that somehow it would save him. Sensing in him this driven quality, this dedication, his classmates treated him with respect, and the activist students let up, apart from occasional threats from a few militants, which seemed more routine and mechanical than real.

But the uneasy peace did not hold for long. He had been back in class for two months when a boycott was called to protest what had now become the daily presence of troops in the township, and to demand the release of student leaders still being held in jail.

"Get the troops out of the township," a spokesman for the Parents' Crisis Committee declared, "and we'll get the children back into the classrooms."

"Get the children back to school first, put a stop to their wildness and lawlessness, and we will remove the troops," the authorities responded.

But the terms of the demands were set by the students, and the parents could not negotiate any settlement without their consent.

The schools remained closed.

There was no way for Tengo to approach his teachers for individual tutoring because that would be regarded by the militant students as a way of defying the boycott. Parents worried about their children missing school but went in fear of the threats of the comrades, and they had no choice but to allow their children to stay away. Winter came on, and in the cold gray of the dawn, workers pushed their way onto the crowded buses and trains, their hearts loaded with anxiety about their children left to roam the township without schooling or supervision.

Desperate with worry, Tengo went to Reverend Gilbert for help. The exams were a few months away. The minister helped him draw up a work schedule and arranged for him to come to him regularly for supervision. But Tengo no longer felt in control; his confidence in himself was slipping away.

The enforced absence from school reminded him of the long drought, when the workers who would have been laboring in the fields were forced to stand by idle and watch the crops wither in the parched earth. It was as though he was waiting for the rain.

He began to spend more and more time with Emma Mbada, the girl in his class who was also planning to go to college. She had suggested they try studying together during the boycott. Since she was top of the class in science and math, and he in English and history, they could help each other, she said. They did not want the others to know they were keeping up with their studies, and Tengo would take a roundabout route to her house. She was an only child. Her mother was a nurse in a clinic in the township, her father a clerk with a law firm in Johannesburg; with both of them away all day, it was peaceful in the small, neat house. There was even a flowerbed in the patch of front garden, where the hot colors of zinnias and marigolds burned bright in the clear winter sunlight.

Tengo and Emma started off studying conscientiously, working their way chapter by chapter through their textbooks, solving algebra and geometry problems with the aid of an answer manual Reverend Gilbert had got hold of for them. But the boycott dragged on and on, and the work they were doing seemed to have less and less reference to anything out in the township or in the world. They were not even sure that they would be allowed by the comrades to sit the matriculation examination at the end of the year. And a day came when they talked, and they touched, and the books no longer seemed as im-

portant or interesting as the two of them suddenly became to each other.

After a time their study sessions became only the
excuse for them to spend time with each other; and as
the months went by they gave up even the pretense of
opening their books. All reference to the matric, to the
future, dropped from their talk. Suspended in a present
without promise, without a likelihood of what they had
both spent many years striving for, they consoled themselves with each other, in the silent house; while outside,
beyond the bravely blooming flowerbed, the order they
longed for was ebbing from their lives, and breakdown
and anarchy were taking over.

Gangs of tsotsis, seizing on the disorder, used it as an
opportunity for criminal activities, looting, smashing,
stoning white drivers of cars passing along the highway,
stealing cars and taking them for wild joyrides before
setting them on fire in the township streets.

Tengo found himself withdrawing more and more
into a state of depression. Only when he was alone in her
house with Emma was he able to forget for a while the
turmoil that had taken over the township and his hopes
for the future. Away from Emma, he spent the days and
nights with a sense of helpless loss, as though someone
had died.

In his pocket was a letter from his mother that he had
put off answering:

> So long as the schools remain closed and you are
> unable to write matric, come home, my boy. The
> oubaas will give you work on the farm, and you can
> go back when the trouble in the township is over.
> It is a long time since you have breathed the good
> fresh air of the country. Your grandmother is get-

ting very old and she longs to see you. So does Tandi.
She is a big girl now. She is still very thin but
thank God she keeps well now and the doctor sees
no sign of the T.B. at present. She must still be
watched in case it comes again. Last week was the
funeral for old Ezekiel. The kraal will not be the
same place now he is gone. He always asked how
you were progressing at school, and said that you
were going to bring us much pride and satisfaction.
As for your father and me—our hearts are longing
for the sight of you. . . .

Remembering the smell of the air at the kraal, the
sun coming up and going down in grandeur over the
rolling veld, the feel of the cow's hide against his cheek
as he pulled the milk down spurting into the bucket,
Tengo ached with his whole being to be at the farm.
But he could not bring himself to go. He was waiting—
waiting. He did not know for what, but he knew he
must wait.

There was a great crisis in his aunt's house when Miriam,
his fifteen-year-old cousin, was found to be pregnant. His
aunt wept with despair. "This is not what we wanted
for you," she moaned. "If they had not shut the schools
down, such a thing would not have happened."

She was not the only mother crying. Many of the
young people, unable to go to school, bored, with nothing
to do, were getting into trouble, and the parents returned
each night to the township filled with apprehension at
what the day might have brought.

When Tengo heard what had happened to Miriam, he
abruptly stopped seeing Emma. The brief spring came

on, quickly followed by the burning heat of summer,
and he lay on his bed or roamed the township alone,
with nothing now to distract him from his hopelessness.
When Emma came to see him to ask why he kept away
from her, he muttered sullenly, not looking at her, "It's
no use. There is no way we can try to make our lives a
little bit better without paying a terrible price."

"You and me?" she asked.

"You and me. All black people. Do you know Miriam
is going to have a baby?" he blurted. He said nothing
more. He lay on his bed staring at the ceiling; he knew
she had left by the sound of the gate clicking shut.

He was supposed to see Reverend Gilbert every week
to report on his progress, but he had stopped going. On
Sundays, when his aunt went to church, she returned
with messages from the minister. But for Tengo, facing
the minister meant facing up to his own loss of hope, and
he was not prepared for the pain this would bring. So
he kept away, not answering the door when he saw
through the window that it was the minister who
knocked, dodging around corners if he spotted him on
the street.

December came and went—the month when the matriculation examination was written throughout the country. In some of the black townships where there was less
unrest, a few students took the exam under pressure
from their parents, with army guards standing by to
prevent activists from disrupting the proceedings. In
other places students were forced by a police ruling to
attend school and take the exam; but many of them,
refusing to write examinations with troops and police
in the classrooms, merely filled their papers with scrib-
bling or with slogans of defiance.

Hearing all this, reading about it in the newspapers, Tengo thought of the terrible dilemma for parents, who, wanting an education for their children and insisting that they write the exams, would make them vulnerable then to retribution by the leaders of the boycott.

In Tengo's township there had been no school for almost a year now, and the time for the matriculation examination came and went, no different from the empty, violence-filled days before and after.

A group of student leaders was released from jail, Elijah and Alice among them. Elijah came to visit Tengo and found him lying on his bed reading a thriller.

A flicker of uneasiness stirred Tengo's heart when his friend walked into the bedroom. He sat up. "Elijah! Man! Are you okay?"

Elijah looked thin but seemed to have lost none of his restless energy. "Oh, man, Tengo. I tell you, it's good to be out of that hell-hole. I'm okay, man. You're not looking too good yourself." He sat down on a chair beside the bed.

"Was it very bad in there?" Tengo forced himself to ask.

"I was lucky. I got pushed around a bit—nothing serious. Alice is okay too. But some of the others— I can tell you stories, man—what they're doing to school kids. . . . A boy in the cell with us, fourteen years old— They picked him up for stoning cars. They whipped him with the sjambok. Sjamboks have steel tips, you know. . . . Another kid, also fourteen—they electrocuted him under his fingernails. And a girl of twelve—she was running home from the bread shop, and a policeman ordered her to stop. She was scared and just kept running—and he shot her in the back!"

Tengo remained silent as Elijah talked on. "Now I hear that at last those Boers in the Dutch Reformed Church have seen the light but it's come too late to save them. They've discovered that it's not written in the Bible that they have to oppress the blacks." Elijah laughed. "But it won't change anything. It's all words, all words."

Tengo waited, knowing that Elijah had come with a purpose. At last he came to the point. "Tengo. The comrades have asked me to speak to you. We think it's time now for you to join the struggle. We left you alone up till now, to finish your studies. But God alone knows when there will be a chance for you to write matric. And there are urgent things to be done now, brother. We have to organize. Either they give in to our demands, or we make the townships ungovernable. They *have got to understand* that we have the power to bring the whole country to a standstill. We need someone like you. You have brains, you write well, you can contribute a lot to the movement."

In Tengo's continuing silence Elijah went on, "Understand, we're not threatening you. We're *asking* you to join us."

"I have to think," Tengo answered.

"I hear from the others that no one sees you. You never go out. I know you want to study—it's a hard deal for you. But these are exciting times, man. We *can* make things change. So since the boycott has prevented you from staying committed to your studies, better commit yourself to our cause, my friend. You look terrible, man. Come out, and I'll buy you a beer and we can talk."

Being let out of jail appeared to have released in Elijah a great spurt of purposeful energy which Tengo envied.

"Thanks, Elijah. I'm not in the mood. But I know I have to do something," he said, morose. "I can't go on like this much longer. Give me time to think it over, man. Give me time. . . ."

Elijah stood up to go. "Don't take too long, my friend. History's on our side now. Things are moving fast. Our time has come, Tengo. It's here. *Now.* We must grab it." He thrust out his hand with a swift, grabbing motion. "Time is running out now for the whites." He took hold of Tengo's shoulder, gripping him as if he wanted to transfuse some of his energy and enthusiasm into the slumped figure sitting on the edge of the bed. "Our time is here—believe me, brother."

Tengo knew what prevented him from making the move Elijah asked of him. He knew that once he made that move, it would mean letting go of his dream; it would mean having to accept the bleak fact that his hope of going on to college was over and done with, that his compelling need to *know*—to try to understand something of the workings of the world—would have to remain with him always like unappeased hunger. And he was unable to bring himself to face that reality.

He spent a lot of time in the next weeks sleeping, and in his waking hours he felt oppressed by a heavy fatigue. Rising late one morning after everyone had left the house, he went to the kitchen to make himself a cup of tea. As he passed through the living room he was startled to see a figure completely covered by a blanket lying on the couch. He went up to it. The person was sound asleep, breathing regularly. He lifted a corner of the blanket. "Joseph!" he whispered, astounded.

It was almost a year since Joseph had been home, and

there had been no word from him. He was in a deep sleep and did not stir while Tengo quietly drank his tea in the kitchen, went out to the yard to wash, and sat down in the living room with a book.

It was past midday when Joseph woke at last. He sat up, threw the blanket aside, yawned, then noticed Tengo watching him. He rubbed the top of his head and smiled. "Hau, Tengo! Greetings, cousin."

"*Joseph.*" Tengo went over and sat down beside him on the couch. "When did you get back? How is it with you? Would you like some tea?"

"A large mug of tea—and something to eat. Is there bread in the house?"

Tengo made tea and a cheese sandwich and brought them to Joseph, aware of a feeling of gladness for the first time in a long while. He watched as his cousin ate and drank. "Man, it's good to see you, Joseph. I hope you don't have to leave right away."

Joseph laughed. "No. I'm staying for a while. But how are things with you, Tengo? Have you been sick?"

Tengo shook his head. "I'm okay," he mumbled.

Joseph gave him a quizzical look. "Well, then tell me what's been happening. I've heard only rumors, but it sounds as if things are boiling up. Tell me everything."

At last here was someone to whom Tengo could unburden his heart.

Joseph sat in silence when Tengo had finished describing to him the events of the past year. "It's amazing," he said. "It's gathering its own momentum. There's no stopping it now." His eyes glowed as if they were looking beyond the small room, the mean house, the battle-scarred township. But as Tengo remained silent, down-cast, Joseph's face became grave. "And you, cousin, you haven't had school for a whole year?"

Tengo shook his head.

Joseph sat in silence. "So you didn't get to write your matric then," he said at last.

"No."

"Hau!" Joseph shook his head. "I'm really very sorry, cousin. It's a terrible shame that you have been caught this way, as if there is not already enough waste, enough bitterness. And all the time I was thinking you would be in college by now. Casualties—casualties," he said as though to himself. "We are fighting a war, and every-where there are casualties. . . ." He thumped Tengo's knee with his fist and said, "We have to talk about the future, cousin. But first"—he pointed outside to the tap and outhouse in the yard—"I must go and avail myself of the luxurious and hygienic toilet facilities supplied to us by our generous municipality. Be a pal, Tengo— make some more tea."

The cousins sat opposite each other at the small plastic-topped metal table in the kitchen.

"Well, Tengo, I think the time has come for me to explain to you what I am doing . . . my work."

A thrill of fear chilled Tengo's back; what he had al-ways wanted to know but now preferred not to hear, Joseph was starting to tell him.

"It is for your ears only, cousin. What you're going to hear you must never tell to another living soul, no matter what anyone tries to do to you. Promise."

"Promise," Tengo said, his mouth dry.

"You can never tell because the safety of many others depends on your silence. I tell you because you have my deepest trust. Okay?"

"Okay."

Now Joseph told him that he was an organizer for the African National Congress, the A.N.C.—the exiled black organization whose leader, Nelson Mandela, had been in jail for over twenty years. Their members were forced to live outside the country and try to organize the resistance to apartheid from afar. Joseph said that he worked for them as a courier and as a recruiter.

"A recruiter?" Tengo asked. "For what?"

"Freedom fighters," Joseph said simply. He sugared his tea heavily, stirred it. "You know, Tengo, that the A.N.C. has always been against violence. At first they sought change by peaceful means. But look where that has got us." He pointed out the window as two armored police trucks lumbered past the house skirting the charred remains of a burned-out bus. "So now we have young people crossing over the border into Zambia and going to join the A.N.C. in Lusaka in order to train as freedom fighters."

Tengo had heard rumors of this. "And you're an organizer?"

Joseph nodded. "They have to be smuggled across the border. It's illegal—and dangerous. But so far our record is pretty good."

"You think I should become a *freedom fighter*?" Tengo asked. He could feel his heart thumping with apprehension.

"Wait, cousin. Not so fast. Listen to me first. When these young people get to Lusaka, the A.N.C. offers them three possibilities: First, they offer schooling to those who want it; second, they offer the opportunity to learn a trade; and third, for those who choose neither of these—"

"They offer military training," Tengo said in a low voice.

Joseph nodded. "That's right. Most of them say that they want to become fighters; they want to work for the revolution so that there will be training and education for everyone. But the leaders try to encourage some of them to go for schooling. They know that we will need skilled, educated people when the time comes. So—"

Now Tengo's heart was beating rapidly. "Joseph, do you think I could—"

"That is exactly what I am thinking, cousin. I think that would be the best thing for you. They send students to schools overseas. You might even have to learn a foreign language to do your studies in, depending on where you land up."

That country on the other side of the sea . . . that he and Frikkie had talked about . . . two small boys on the bank of the river, with the willow branches overhanging the water where small silvery fish flickered in the shallows. . . . "*Overseas*," Tengo said softly. "Joseph, would that *really* be possible?" he asked, feeling a stir of promise under the hopelessness that had weighed on him for so long.

"Oh, it's more than possible, cousin. It's going on all the time. But it's not easy. If you get to Lusaka in one piece, and you're sent to a foreign country, then it's something else. It's cold . . . and strange. The skies in foreign countries are nearly always gray. You're far away from your friends and family. And the food they eat is different. And even though there is no apartheid, you still feel an outsider, a foreigner, lonely. . . ."

"*Joseph*," Tengo whispered, the skin on his scalp and

neck and shoulders prickling and tingling, "Joseph, you've *been* overseas."

Joseph's eyes regarded Tengo across the top of the chipped enamel mug he was drinking from.

"Joseph, *where?*"

Joseph finished his tea and put down the mug. "Ask me no questions, Tengo. The less you know, the safer you are. I'm telling you all this because it is not a decision you can make without giving it a lot of thought. It's not easy. You will get an education—free. Your living expenses will be paid, but it's only a small stipend. Those who are doing it, their stomachs are not always full. And it can be cold and lonely. They begin to long for home even under *these conditions.*" He pointed with his thumb over his shoulder to the blackened skeleton of the overturned bus out on the road.

Tengo's eyes followed the gesture; he noticed a large sheet of bright pink plastic that had blown and been caught in the smashed windshield, flapping desolately in the breeze.

"I must be honest with you and warn you it will be hard, Tengo, so that you can ask yourself—is it worth it?" He reached into his shirt pocket for a cigarette and lit it.

Across the table an ant made its way, laboriously carrying a spilled grain of sugar. They watched it as it came to the table's edge; while carefully scouting the downward descent it lost its hold on the sugar grain, which fell to the floor. The ant remained poised for a moment, rubbing its empty front legs together, before scurrying to the corner and descending by way of the table leg.

"Good luck, ant," Joseph said. He poured more tea from the dented tin teapot, added evaporated milk from a pierced can, stirred in sugar. "Here I come back from

my trip thinking that my clever cousin is already busy
getting his B.A. And what do I find? No school, no
matric, the whole township trashed. I can't blame the
kids for wanting to *destroy*. All their energy has nowhere to go except to turn into hate and anger. I would
have been the same if I hadn't got caught up in the
struggle. It's hard to keep your bitterness at the way the
system treats us from turning into hatred for the whites.
And now the police are making it their job to keep our
hatred burning hot all the time. But you're a gentle
person, Tengo. The A.N.C., you'll find when you get to
Lusaka—*if* you decide to go, I mean—the A.N.C. believes
that blacks and whites have *got* to live together in this
country. We need them. They need us. The Freedom
Charter of the A.N.C. *states* that South Africa belongs to
all who live in it—black and white."

"Do you hate whites, Joseph?"

"Do I hate whites?" Joseph lifted his head and blew
out a plume of smoke, watching it as it dissolved around
the bare bulb of the light fitting. "No, Tengo. I'm not
anti-white. There are whites working with us: The
women of the Black Sash. They're tough and brave; right
now they're investigating and exposing some of the
torture that's going on in the jails. And there are others
—university students, lawyers. There are white doctors
who are privately treating some of the comrades when
they're wounded by the police, so that they don't have
to go to hospital where the doctors are obliged to report
all bullet wounds to the authorities. There's the cam-
paign against conscription. . . ."

"There's Reverend Gilbert," Tengo said.

"Yes. And others like him in religious organizations.
They are the hope we have, to try and work things out
with *them* when our time comes."

"But when is our time coming?" Tengo asked, feeling low again. "How long will it take? How much more killing and smashing, burning and school boycotting?"

"We don't ask that question. We just do what needs to be done. We are in a state of revolution, Tengo, and there is more hardship and suffering ahead. Much more. But we will win. We don't ask how long. It will take as long as it takes to win."

Tengo looked at his cousin, feeling a sense of awe at the thought that he had actually been there, been *overseas*. It seemed to weight his words with added authority. "Do you have to leave soon?"

"I will be here about a month if all goes according to schedule. And you—you have a month to think, and to make up your mind about what you want to do. Now I have work to do. Tell me—Elijah Mphlane—we heard he was arrested."

"He's out now. His sister too. He has been trying to get me to join in with the comrades."

"He's a good fellow, Elijah. Tengo, before I go—remember, talk of what I have told you to no one. *No one.* There are informers everywhere."

"I've been wondering about that, Joseph. Why are black people informers? Why would black people want to cooperate with the authorities when they see them beating and shooting and jailing blacks day after day?"

Joseph frowned, drummed his fingers on the table. "People become informers because they are hungry, or greedy, or afraid. Or because they or their families have been threatened by the police. Or because they can only care about the good of their own family, and they can't extend their concern as far as the good of their neighbors or their community or the suffering of other people.

When I was a youngster, I once asked Reverend Gilbert the same question."

"What did he say?"

"He said that human beings are frail, and afraid, and perplexed. Well, that's true, but it's not enough. We're also each responsible for what we do. And we're responsible for one another." He pushed back his chair and stood up. "I'd like to sit here all day discussing philosophy with you, cousin. But I have work to do. See you later!"

Tengo heard the clatter of the front gate as it banged shut behind his cousin. He sat on at the table, thinking about their talk.

C H A P T E R

15

*F*or the first few days after Joseph's return Tengo went about filled with elation. He began to get up early in the mornings. He helped the old woman clean and tidy the house. He ironed his clothes instead of pulling them stiff and crinkled off the line and stepping into them.

He watched Joseph's coming and going with a feeling of glad anticipation that he had not experienced for a long time. Joseph could save him; it was in his power to get him away from here, from the squalor and ugly dread that flared like smoky fires at the sight of the police and soldiers patrolling the streets. Through Joseph the books, the teachers, the instruction that gave life order and meaning for him would be available again.

He saw to it that there was food for Joseph at whatever odd hour he came in. He offered to wash and iron his clothes when he did his own. He gave up reading thrillers and went back to finishing *The Mill on the Floss*, which was one of the matric textbooks. He carried his gladness around with him like a concealed treasure.

He went to visit Emma one day. He could see she was surprised to see him, but she remained wary, distant. She hadn't forgiven him for the break in their friendship. The sun glared from a cloudless sky. She offered him a cool drink but did not invite him in, and brought out two bottles of lemonade, which they drank sitting on the front doorstep. Beside the step a cement flower urn spilled over with bright orange nasturtiums among round flat saucerlike leaves; there had been a thunder shower in the night, and the silvery raindrops cupped in the leaves shimmered in the sunlight; the fresh smell of dampened earth rose from the flowerpot.

Emma glanced sideways at him. "You're looking pleased with yourself," she remarked, keeping her distance.

"Oh, I'm not too bad now," he answered. "I was feeling pretty awful for a long time. But now perhaps— well, who knows?"

"You're going away," she said with a sharp intake of breath.

He lifted his head and emptied the bottle of soda, feeling its cold prickly sweetness run down his throat. He thought, I must be careful not to say anything.

Out on the pavement a small boy ran by rolling the metal rim of a bicycle wheel along with a stick; a smaller child dressed only in a shrunken T-shirt toddled behind him, crying, trying to catch up with him.

"How about you, Emma? Have you been doing any studying?"

She looked sullen. "I've kept up with my work. My parents have managed to get me into Richmond."

"Richmond? What's that?"

"It's that private multiracial school outside Jo'burg. I'm starting there when the new term begins. The headmaster says I can write my matric at the end of next year. Then I'm going to college. I want to be a lawyer."

"You're lucky. I wish my parents could afford private school for me."

"Money wouldn't help. Since the school boycott they've had hundreds of applications. They haven't got any room. But my parents put my name down long ago, so I was one of the few they could take."

"Well, I'm glad for you, Emma." He put his hand on her arm but she shook it off. He felt himself bursting to tell her of his new possibilities, to explain that it was his hopelessness that had kept him away from her, that now there seemed to be a future again. But Joseph had told him he could speak of it to no one. She looked hurt and unfriendly. She had carefully plucked a nasturtium leaf with a raindrop in the hollow near the stem; she held it cupped in her hand, moving the round perfect drop so that it caught the light as it trembled like a blob of mercury on the surface of the leaf.

"When I was a kid, on the farm," Tengo said, "this boy, Frikkie—the nephew of the oubaas—and I, we used to play together. We had a game we would play with these leaves. We would each have a leaf with a raindrop in it, and we would run round and round and round the house to see who could keep going the longest without spilling the drop."

Emma twirled the leaf by its stem. The drop fell off, and she crumpled the leaf and threw it away. The pungent smell of the juice of the leaf took Tengo back for a keen, vivid moment to the madam's flowerbed at the farm.

He stood up to go. "Well, thanks for the cold drink.

I'll see you." He went off. Before turning the corner he looked back and saw her standing in the doorway, watching him, the two empty bottles dangling from her hands.

Late one night Tengo sat at his desk reading by the light of the tiny, high-intensity lamp the minister had given him to study by when he had first come to school. On two of the four beds crowded into the room, one of his uncles and a cousin from the country were asleep. The uncle snored softly.

Tengo concentrated on the annotated edition of the Shakespeare play he was working his way through: *Julius Caesar*. He had returned to his matric textbooks and was studying long hours each day. "I don't want my brain to go rusty before I can get back to school again," he'd told Joseph.

Joseph was still out. There was a pot of *putu*—sour porridge—and some stew that his aunt had left on the stove. He would heat it up for Joseph when he got back.

Long after midnight the door opened softly and Joseph came in. To Tengo's surprise, Elijah was with him. "We've eaten," Joseph whispered, "but let's have some tea, cousin."

Tengo made the tea while Joseph and Elijah sat at the table speaking in low voices.

"Has anyone actually *seen* Benny?" Joseph asked.

"Yes. Msona saw him. He slept over at their place for a couple of nights. Then his auntie gave him the money to go back to his parents' kraal. Msona says he looks terrible."

Tengo put the cups and the tin of condensed milk on

the table. In the weak light from the bare bulb over the kitchen table he could see that his cousin looked worried.

"Did he say *why* he came back?" Joseph asked.

"He said he just couldn't take it any longer," Elijah answered with a shrug. "He said he tried. He said people were good to him. Kind. But they couldn't understand what he was going through. He had difficulty learning to speak the language. But he said the worst thing was the cold and the short days. He thought he would go mad if he didn't see the sun. He couldn't sleep. He began to have nightmares, and the student he was sharing with complained he was being kept awake every night. Anyway, they decided to send him back. They said he would have a nervous breakdown if he stayed."

Joseph looked grave. "It's a real shame. I would have thought Benny was one of the tough ones. You can never tell how a person is going to stand up to it."

"Well," Elijah said, "he said if you've lived your whole life in the township, you can't imagine how it will be overseas. He said it was the loneliness. Sometimes he felt like crying when he just thought about the taste of putu with meat. He said he was afraid that his tongue would forget how to speak Xhosa."

As he listened, Tengo felt doubt creeping into his heart. They were talking of someone who had been sent *overseas* to study. *Whoever Benny is*, he thought, *what has happened with him could happen with me too if I go overseas. . . .*

"But *you* know how it is, Joseph," Elijah went on. "You've been through it yourself."

"Yes. It's true what he says. But it was different for me," Joseph answered. "I knew it would only be one year.

Benny was supposed to be three, four years there. That's a different story."

"You shouldn't feel bad about this, Joseph. You can't be responsible for everything," Elijah said.

"I recommended him," Joseph replied.

"Don't worry. He's a good fellow, Benny. When he comes back, Sizwe says he can work with the youth council he's trying to set up. Sizwe's idea is, that once we have made the township ungovernable, and the police and the army can't control things any longer, we must already have set up the organization to govern the township on our own—without white interference. There are plans to set up people's courts to keep day-by-day life orderly; there are plans to try to influence the gangs of tsotsis to work with us in this, plans to come up with alternate school courses—"

"What troubles me—" Joseph cut in, "is that as more and more of our leaders in the youth movement are being arrested, we are going to lose control over the anger of the kids. Violence is an everyday business in the townships now. Without leadership, the comrades could start behaving like the tsotsis."

"It worries me too," Elijah said. "There were some kids yesterday at the meeting—" he lowered his voice, "they were maybe twelve, thirteen years old. And they were talking about putting the 'necklace' on someone. . . ."

A pang of horror went through Tengo. The *necklace*—the dreaded punishment inflicted on those considered enemies of the struggle: a tire filled with petrol placed around the victim's neck and set alight. . . .

"You'll be seeing Sizwe tomorrow," Elijah went on. "This is a serious problem the committee needs to discuss." He drank up his tea and rose to go. "I must get some sleep, comrade. Thanks for the tea, Tengo." He clasped Tengo by the shoulder and looked directly into his face. "It is good that you are going to be one of us, brother. Joseph has told me that you are ready to go."

Elijah's clear, frank gaze was unnerving. Tengo said yes in a low voice and moved away to clear the table.

Now Tengo's brief period of gladness was over. Joseph tumbled into bed and was asleep at once. For Tengo there was no sleep. The conversation between Elijah and Joseph in the kitchen had chilled his heart over—like the ice that formed on a bucket of water left standing outside the dairy on a winter's night. He had wanted so desperately to go on with his studies that he had jumped at Joseph's suggestion—at the idea of *overseas*—without allowing himself to think what it would mean—to go and live in a strange, cold country, a foreign land. Eastern Europe and Sweden were the places that made education available to young black South Africans, Joseph had told him.

But now he admitted to himself that he had not thought clearly about it. He had imagined, like a child, a fabled place on the other side of the sea where everything that was wrong and unfair and cruel here would be right and fair and kind. He had looked in his atlas at the maps of Eastern Europe and Sweden and had seen himself there in orderly classrooms and splendid libraries where scholars spoke in hushed voices. He saw himself now—a forlorn, desolate figure walking alone over the wastes of pink and green of the atlas, with the thin lines that were meant to be rivers running everywhere like cracks, and black dots for cities. . . . He groaned in the dark. The price, always so high for the things he wanted, was too high—more than he could afford. Whoever Benny was, his experience overseas struck recognition in Tengo as if he had been through it himself. You can never tell how a person will stand up to it, Joseph had said in the kitchen. Better to admit to himself *now* that he was not one of the tough ones. Overseas—lonely and a stranger— was not for him. He would have to give up the idea of continuing his education.

There was nothing for him but to learn to do without those things his spirit yearned for, in the same way he had learned to do without sufficient clothes and food and books. He would have to train himself, the way he had trained his fingers to forget their yearning for the feel of a lump of pliable clay and the promise of what lay concealed within it.

There was no escape from what the system had prepared for him. He could only join in now with the others.

He fell asleep as the gray dawn crept over the township, his decision made. He would say nothing of his change of mind to Joseph. He would go with him; he would slip over the border with him to Lusaka. When he got there, he would choose to undergo the military training the African National Congress offered; he would become a freedom fighter rather than undertake to become a lonely black student in a strange cold country. When his training was completed, he would come back, and he would do what needed to be done.

Later that week Tengo lay awake listening for Joseph. He worried always, now, that his cousin might be arrested. There had been a new government crackdown: Reporting of disturbances or protest was banned from the news; political activists were being arrested all across the country; thousands of children were picked up by the police; some were beaten and released, but most of them were being kept indefinitely in jail, some of them tortured and abused. Every day in the township anguished parents were turned away from the police station when they tried to find out where their children were. While Tengo had been fixing the wash-line post that afternoon, he had heard the woman next door loudly weeping. She had been hoping, he knew, that the Detainees Parents Committee might be able to help her find out what had happened to her thirteen-year-old son, and she had just learned from them that the authorities were refusing to give out any information on the whereabouts of jailed children. Through the wire fence Tengo had watched the ten-year-old daughter trying to quiet her two small brothers who kept up a dismal wailing at their mother's distress; he had tried offering them an orange, but they would not be comforted.

At last he heard the door open and Joseph come in. He slipped out of bed and handed him a letter addressed to him that had been left under the door during the afternoon. Joseph glanced at the envelope. "Thanks, cousin. Is there something to eat? I'm empty." He patted his stomach.

In the kitchen, while Tengo heated the food, Joseph read the letter. He replaced it in the envelope, struck a match, and held it to one corner, watching the creeping flame as it blackened and consumed it. He dropped the charred paper into an ashtray and watched as the last corner curled crisply up and the flame died down. Then he took a cigarette from the pack in his shirt pocket and lit up, inhaling deeply.

Tengo set the plate of food down in front of him. After a few more puffs Joseph stubbed out the cigarette, examined it to make sure it was cold, and replaced it in the pack. He ate in silence. When Tengo brought him his tea, he took out the half-smoked butt, relit it, leaned back in his chair, and said, "We leave at the beginning of next week, cousin."

"*Next week!*" Tengo whispered.

"I can't say exactly which day yet. Hold yourself ready. Pack just a few things—essentials. We must travel light."

"Can I write to my parents that I'm going away?"

"No. Nothing. Not a word. No one."

The seriousness and composure with which Joseph had read and destroyed the letter and announced the plan impressed Tengo and reassured him. He saw him now as a leader rather than the beloved cousin he had taught to swim all those years ago in the little river on the farm of the oubaas.

While Tengo felt confident in placing himself in his cousin's hands, at the same time he was disturbed at the idea of going off without his parents knowing what was happening to him. He thought of the empty space he would leave by not saying good-bye to his aunt and relatives, and he felt troubled as he realized the burden of anxiety his disappearance would lay on his mother. He regretted now that he had not been back to the kraal to visit them.

He woke early the next morning in a turmoil of excitement and trepidation. Joseph had already gone out. Before breakfast Tengo washed his clothes and hung them out on the line. He finished his tea and bread, then sorted through his possessions stored under the bed in the cardboard suitcase he had brought when he left the kraal. He went through his books, wondering if Joseph would allow him to take one or two along. He laid aside a paperback copy of *The Story of Art* by Gombrich that Claire had given him. She had used it in her studies, and many of the pages were underlined in yellow marker. He had leafed through it from time to time but had been saving it up like treasure, to be read after he had written his matric. If he were allowed one book, this would be the one he would pack in the green nylon backpack that was all the luggage he was taking. He set aside a small pile of books to be returned to Reverend Gilbert.

It was a hot windy morning, and his clothes were soon dry. He ironed and folded them and put them on the shelf above his bed, ready to be stowed into the pack as soon as Joseph gave him the word; it would not do to draw any attention to his intended departure.

He waited until late afternoon before setting out for the church hall to return Reverend Gilbert's books. The minister would most likely have gone home by then; it would be better not to see him than to have to lie or be evasive about what he was planning to do. He would have liked to tell the minister that he had chosen to join the struggle, though he would be disappointed to hear Tengo was giving up his studies. He would have liked to thank him for being like a father to him all the years in the township. But Joseph had told him, *Nothing—not a word—No one.*

As he neared the center of the township he heard shouts and saw people running. A yellow bus with riot policemen peering through wire-mesh-protected windows cruised slowly past. Tengo walked on, buoyed by the knowledge that soon he would be away from all this, that his time of waiting, with its emptiness and bitterness and waste, would soon be over. He considered nothing now beyond escaping the desolation of the township.

The minister's secretary was just about to close up the office when he got there. She seemed agitated as she took the books from him.

"Has the reverend gone home?" he asked.

"No. He went to the funeral." She locked the office door.

The funeral—Tengo remembered then, with some guilt. He was conscious suddenly of his self-preoccupation. Joseph had said he was going to it—a funeral for seven people, four of them schoolchildren—who had been shot the previous week after stone throwing had broken out when the police had fired on a group holding a protest. Under the state of emergency declared by the government in their effort to quell the continuing unrest, no public gatherings were permitted; since funerals were the only places where people could come together, they had become occasions where speakers denounced the government's treatment of black people.

The secretary walked with Tengo down the steps of the church. "There's going to be trouble," she said. "I must get home quickly and make sure my children are indoors."

"What have you heard?" he asked her.

"They've been forbidden to hold a rally after the burials. But they're going to have it. Reverend Gilbert had a call from town to say the army is coming to break it up." She hurried off down the street.

As she walked away, Tengo heard the swelling rise and fall of a great crowd chanting. From the steps of the church, which was built on a slope, he had a view across the township. He saw a slow-moving mass of people winding its way up the road, flowing on like a tide released into a narrow channel. As they came nearer, he saw that many of them held up banners and placards calling for an end to the killing of children and demanding the withdrawal of soldiers and police from the township. Some were waving the black, green, and gold flag of the A.N.C. They approached, chanting and leaping and dancing in the manner of a tribal dance, shouting "*Amandla! Amandla! Power!*"

People near the church were pointing and gesticulating, and Tengo turned his head and saw, on the road beyond one of the guarded main entrances to the township, a line of greenish-brown army vehicles approaching. Chanting and dancing, the crowd coursed in from the opposite direction into the central area in front of the church. Like a slow-moving centipede the line of armored trucks slid in through the gates and twisted its way up the side streets and into the area surrounding the church. They drew to a halt, and soldiers in battle dress jumped down and stood with their guns at the ready.

From the top of the leading vehicle a senior officer emerged, holding up an electronic megaphone, and Tengo heard the harsh consonants and hoarse gutturals of Afrikaans echo out over the housetops. "This is an illegal gathering. You are ordered to disperse *at once. At once!* You have precisely *two minutes* to disperse." The injunction was repeated in English, but within seconds, before the meaning of the words could be taken in or those caught in the crush could move off into the surrounding streets, there was a burst of firing.

In the gathering dusk panic broke out, the air filled with terror as people were hit and fell and the dense crowd tried to scatter out of the range of the bullets. The great tide of people surged in all directions, and the soldiers, finding themselves marooned like a small island in a vast threatening sea, opened fire again. Motionless on the steps, Tengo saw more people fall, shot in the back as they fled down a side street.

Suddenly, from an area at the side of the church hall, a hail of stones came flying through the air, striking many of the soldiers. They were being hurled, Tengo could see, by a group of boys and girls, teenagers, who were making no effort to escape and who yelled imprecations as their crude ammunition flew through the air. There was a barked command from the officer in charge; canisters of tear gas were sent spinning overhead and exploded in suffocating clouds that thickened the dusk.

Jostling, butting, and screaming, people panicked as they tried to escape the choking, smarting fumes. But from the side of the church hall there came a renewed barrage of bricks and stones. A soldier was hit. Blood spurted from his brow. Shots rang out and Tengo saw two of the teenagers fall and lie sprawled on the ground.

Standing on the steps, he had been watching the confrontation with stunned horror. The chaos and blood-spilling and terror had erupted in the space of a few minutes. Now the anger that was lying coiled and waiting in him quickened and impelled him around the side of the church to the piece of waste ground from where the rocks were still flying. Here, where the ground was littered with broken bricks and masonry and lumps of rubble, with a sensation as if his rage were taking wing, he picked up and started to fling at the soldiers whatever he could lay his hands on. With each rock he hurled, something that had lain mute and ugly and dangerous at the root of his being rose up and flew out, released, bitterly gratifying. Coughing and choking, his eyes on fire from the tear gas, Tengo flung the rocks one after the other, experiencing as each one soared its arc through the air a sense of freedom he had never known.

Now three soldiers came running toward the rubble-strewn lot. Suddenly, from somewhere behind the lot a single shot rang out, and one of the soldiers fell to the ground.

For an instant Tengo stood still with astonishment. Who in the township had a gun? Who was the crack shot? It was almost impossible for blacks to arm themselves. Their only ammunition was their anger, or petrol and matches, or the rubbish that lay always to hand in the wreckage of their landscape. *Who was the single sniper?* he wondered. *Where had he taken his deadly aim from?*

The two soldiers were bending over their fallen comrade, but, alerted by the solitary crack of the sniper's bullet, two more soldiers appeared and fired a burst into the lot where the youths were gathered.

"Run! Run! Run!" someone yelled. Tengo dropped the lump of concrete he was holding and darted off behind the church hall. A shot whistled past his ankle and hit the ground near his foot. He kept running. He could hear the thud of heavy boots pounding after him. He sprinted around a corner, passing a group of women dipping basins of water from a bucket and pouring it over the head of a tiny child who was rubbing his eyes and screaming at the painful burning of the tear gas.

In the next block of houses a narrow alley ran between the back fences; he slipped into its cover and stopped, listening to hear if he was still being pursued. The idea passed through his mind that perhaps the soldier suspected him of being the sniper. Peering around the side of the house, he saw the soldier talking to the women.

He sped on down the alley, leaping over abandoned mattresses with their stuffing disgorged, broken furniture and overturned rubbish bins, skirting piles of abandoned tires, his eyes smarting and his nostrils filled with the foul rotting smells of the litter of garbage. Panting, he came out onto the road. He stood for a moment to regain his breath. A small girl ran past, crying, clutching a carton of milk, blood pouring down the side of her face. From behind him Tengo heard again the thud of heavy boots.

He could see that the alley continued on the other side of the road, and he took off again, crossing the road into the dark of the narrow passage, dodging past and leaping over the strewn rubbish, tripping and stumbling as he ran. It was getting dark now. He ran on, in his mind a refrain beating in time with his winded breathing: *I mustn't be caught, not now—not now—not when my chance has come to get away from all this. . . .* His feet seemed to pound out as he ran: *I mustn't be caught— not now—not now. . . .*

He was coming to the outskirts of the township, where the houses petered out onto a stretch of veld where the stripped and rusting wreckage of cars lay about like monstrous animal skeletons in the dusk. At the far end of the field there was an abandoned shed made of sheets of corrugated iron that had once been a car repair shop. The door was shut. Tengo pushed against it. It opened, and he slipped inside and closed it behind him.

It was dim inside. Faint light came in through windows opaque with grime. He leaned against the door listening to the knocking of his heart, the sharp intake of his panting breath. As his eyes adjusted to the absence of light, he made out a heap of tires and an overturned metal chair with one leg missing; some sagging sacks were piled in a corner beside a couple of car batteries. Waiting to get his breath back, he stood leaning against the door, the voice in the back of his mind pleading, *not now—not now*. He moved away from the door and stood, listening, against the wall. Some small creature rustled behind the leaning sacks, startling him. From the center of the township came the noise of sporadic firing.

He strained his ears, listening for any sounds from the direction of the alley, wondering if he had shaken his pursuer off. On the floor near the window, next to a couple of kerosene tins, something caught his eye. He went over, picked it up quickly, and returned to his position flattened against the wall beside the door; it was a heavy, short piece of metal, a piece of a broken crowbar. He gripped it firmly in his right hand.

His mouth was dry, his eyes still burning. Close to the door hinge he waited, his fingers clenched on the metal bar, every nerve in him straining with tensed alertness. Outside there was silence.

CHAPTER

16

*S*uddenly, with a crashing sound the door was kicked open. It swung back, hitting Tengo a blow on the forehead. "*Kom buitekant, kaffir!*" a voice shouted. "*Ek weet jy's daar!*"—"Come on out, kaffir! I know you're there!"

Pressed against the wall, Tengo gripped the bar in both hands, barely breathing.

The muzzle of a gun appeared, poking past the edge of the door. Cautiously, preceded by the pointed gun, the soldier took a step over the threshold. One more step brought him beyond the open door; he stood, a shadowy figure, wary, poised.

With a swift, sudden movement Tengo kicked the door shut and stepped forward wielding the bar and striking wildly in the dark. Startled, the soldier yelled, and with a nasty thud the bar made contact; there was a groan and the soldier fell to the floor.

In the silence Tengo thought, *I've killed him—I must get out of here.* But the soldier had dropped in front of the door. Still clutching the iron bar, Tengo bent to move the slumped figure from the doorway. The soldier suddenly spoke. "Don't move, kaffir." His words were thick, mumbled: "Don't move or I'll shoot."

In the dimness of the shed Tengo saw the soldier had raised himself on an elbow and was groping for his gun. Moving quickly, Tengo kicked the gun out of his reach and picked it up.

The soldier groaned and fell back, lying on his side. "Oh God . . ." he said in Afrikaans.

The gun in one hand, the metal bar in the other, Tengo stood over him, shocked at what he had done. The impact of the metal on the bone of the soldier's skull filled him with sick horror. The soldier groaned again. "Don't kill me . . ." he mumbled.

Kill? Tengo wondered: *How could I kill anyone? Yet— he would have killed me.*

Now the soldier lay still and silent. Perhaps I *have* killed him, Tengo thought aghast. Presently the soldier stirred, moaned; with relief Tengo realized he had only fainted.

He had no idea what to do next. He must get away. But the gun . . . If he left it, the soldier would come round and use it again—to kill someone. But if he went outside with a gun in his hand, he would be shot by the first white soldier or policeman he encountered.

He felt suddenly weak, as if his knees had lost solidity. He sat down on one of the kerosene tins and pressed his head down over his lap until the feeling of faintness passed.

The soldier lay motionless on the floor, his arm still outstretched where he had fumbled for his gun. Tengo slipped the metal bar into the belt of his blue jeans, and hefted the gun in his hands, peering closely in the dimness to examine it. He held it as he had seen others hold guns, curling his right forefinger over the trigger, with the muzzle pointing at the soldier. He assumed it must be cocked, and thought, *I suppose if I squeeze it, it will go off.* But he was trapped now, by the gun. He could not take it or leave it, nor did he want to use it—though Joseph or Elijah would probably have no such qualms.

The soldier lay very still. His cap had been knocked off when he fell, and it lay on the floor near his head; his face was in the shadows, but in the glimmer of light that came through the dirty windows Tengo could make out his skull, which was covered with short-cropped very fair hair, the yellow hair of the Boers. Now the soldier was stirring. Tengo tightened his grasp on the gun. The soldier moved his head, raised himself on his elbow, muttered something unintelligible, and sat up groggily. He closed his eyes and clutched the side of his head. "Where am I? . . . What happened? . . ." he murmured, speaking to himself. He opened his eyes and saw his captor sitting a yard away, watching his every movement. "*Eina!*" he groaned, "my head . . ." He moved his eyes and encountered the barrel of the gun. "Oh God . . ." he groaned again and sank back on the floor.

At the sound of the soldier's voice, something stirred in Tengo, hovering just beyond the grasp of memory—something fearful. He felt deeply afraid, as if what he had been running away from all the time—what he had thought school and learning would save him from—was here, in the hut, with him and the white soldier. He felt it stir in him; he could taste it almost, bitter and metallic in his mouth.

On the floor the soldier remained motionless. The first

time Tengo had felt this taste in his mouth he had run from it, run over the veld on a bright winter's day. There were three vultures hanging up in the sky that morning, he remembered. He and Frikkie had watched them. It was a taste he could not identify at the time. But that same winter he had tasted it again; it had risen up, filled his mouth, choking him almost, when a girl with red hair and pale freckles on her white skin had insulted old Ezekiel, speaking to him as if he were a mongrel dog, and he an elder of the tribe.

Now the soldier was muttering again; he moved his head restlessly, and his cheek and profile showed palely in the haze of faint light that filtered in. Sitting on the upturned tin, watching him, Tengo felt his palms go damp and sweaty where they curled around the stock of the gun. The soldier lay at his feet, eyes closed. Tengo dropped onto his knees and bent over the recumbent form, peering into the face, his eyes straining in the dimness. His heart heaved in his chest and he felt the blood drain from his face, leaving him cold and clammy. He sank back on his heels, his tongue rigid in his dry mouth, his throat tight so that words would not come. His voice came up then, on a hoarse outtake of breath. "*Frikkie . . .*" he whispered.

Abruptly, the soldier sat up and looked around, confused.

"Frikkie—" Tengo said again.

"How d'you know my name? Who are you, kaffir?" the soldier said in a fright, raising one knee and pushing himself back along the floor.

Tengo remained silent. Now the soldier leaned forward, peering through the gloom. A contusion was darkening down the side of his head and face, and one eye was closed by swelling. Painfully, he pulled himself closer. "Oh no . . . My God, it's not true. Is it? Is it Tengo?" he asked in a faint voice.

Tengo was standing now, the gun held limply in his right hand, the barrel pointing to the floor.

"Tengo, *so waar*—is it you?" the soldier asked hoarsely.

"It's me."

"What are you doing here? Are you going to kill me? Oh, my head . . ." He moaned again. "Oh, I feel so sick." He drew up his knees, resting his forehead on them, waiting for the waves of nausea to subside.

As if they had a memory of their own, Tengo's hands were recalling the sensation of the blow running through the iron bar from the skull of the soldier into his fingers. Over and over he experienced the force of the blow, each time filled with horror that it was Frikkie's skull on which his hands had brought down the metal.

". . . so thirsty . . . a drink of water," Frikkie was mumbling.

"There's nothing here," Tengo said roughly.

Feebly, Frikkie patted his side. "Here." Tengo saw a flat water bottle strapped to the leather belt. Holding the gun under his arm, he unbuckled the bottle, unstoppered it, and held it out. His head still bent over his knees, Frikkie made no move to take it.

"Here, lift up your head." Tengo held the bottle to his mouth, and Frikkie drank, some of the water spilling down his chin; he wiped it with his sleeve. "Thanks, Tengo."

Now Tengo lifted the bottle and drank, slaking the dryness of his mouth. He put the stopper back and placed the bottle on the floor; then moved back to sit down on the kerosene tin with the gun resting across his lap.

"I can't sit up. I must rest against something," Frikkie

mumbled. He dragged himself a few yards and leaned back against the stacked hessian sacks. They rustled, as if they were stuffed with straw.

There was silence in the shed. Outside a full moon had come up, its pure pale radiance seeming to mock the wretchedness of the township. It cast a slab of ice-blue light across the floor. In the shadows the dark head and the fair head were discernible a couple of yards apart.

After a time Frikkie spoke. "It's Tengo. It's really you, Tengo. I can't believe it. Here we are again—Tengo and Frikkie. I knew you were living near Jo'burg; your mother told me. But I didn't know *this* was your township."

In a turmoil of hostility and regret, Tengo made no reply.

Frikkie rubbed his temple, fingered his swollen eye. "Man, what did you hit me with? My head feels like it's cracked."

"What else could I do?" Tengo blurted out. "You had the gun."

It's Tengo, Frikkie thought to himself. *If I'd only known . . . But when I saw it was Pieter Uys lying there with a bullet in his head . . . Pieter—he's probably dead.* Frikkie groaned out loud. *I thought the kaffir I saw running away must be the killer. Now we're here, the two of us—me and Tengo. Now he has my gun. It's cocked; he can kill me if he wants to. No one knows I'm here.* Tengo can kill me. *But I might have killed him. . . . God . . . my head! He's probably fractured my skull. He hates me. We're enemies. How is it possible,* he wondered, *for Tengo and me to be enemies? We played together from the age of three.* The thought of Oom Koos and the farm rose up in him, filling him with longing.

"Tengo?"

"What?"

"D'you remember that summer when I taught you to swim?"

Tengo made no answer.

"D'you remember, Tengo?"

"Yes. So?"

"So nothing. I just remembered, that's all."

Tengo remembered too—the pleasure, the wallowing about and splashing, fearful he would sink until, miraculously, under Frikkie's shouted instruction and encouragement, he found himself buoyant, supported by water. But he must not think about that time. He could feel himself weakening, losing his grip if he allowed himself to remember. His anger returned.

"The only reason that you could teach me was that you went to school, *free*, and you learned to swim there. There we were—two boys, the same age—and *everything* was there for you because you're white, and nothing for me because I'm black. How do you think that feels? *How do you think that feels?* And when we measured ourselves next to that tree, you were bigger than me. And you told me—you told me that I should eat more mielie-pap," he said bitterly.

Frikkie remained silent, shocked by the outburst. "I'm sorry, Tengo. I didn't mean anything. I was just remembering, that's all—the river, milking the cows, the way we used to run away from Sissie."

"She was a real brat, your sister," Tengo said curtly. He sat with the barrel of the gun across his lap, holding the weapon firmly.

"She's still a pain in the neck. She's training to be a legal secretary."

"Yes," Tengo said. "And *my* sister, Tandi—what's

there for her? She's had T.B. What can *she* look forward
to? Being a maid in your mother's house, cleaning up the
mess of white people—"

Frikkie was slumped against the sacks. His head and
face throbbed painfully. He felt cornered by Tengo's
anger. His words shocked him. They were forbidden
words, things not to be brought up between black and
white. This was the third time his unit had been called
in to quell township unrest, and it had never occurred to
him that among the shouting angry black faces of the
crowds into which he had been trained to aim live ammunition, rubber bullets, buckshot, canisters of tear gas,
one of the faces might be Tengo's. *They don't know how
scared we are*, he thought, *having to jump off the Casspirs into the softness of a crowd of civilians. It was soft,
and frightening—women and girls in their dresses,
schoolchildren, old people. It wasn't . . . firm—war with
armed, uniformed soldiers fighting each other was firm.
Don't they realize how frightening it is to have to plunge
into that soft sea of hate and violence—so many of them
and so few of us even though we have the sticks and guns?
Now Tengo has the gun—and he could kill me. Tengo
could kill me.* But even as he was thinking it, he knew he
did not believe it. He and Tengo . . .

His mouth . . . it was so dry he could feel his tongue
clacking against his palate. "Tengo, give me a drink
of water."

Tengo set the water bottle beside him and sat down
again. *What am I going to do?* he asked himself. The
gloom in the shed was thickening, the small space closing
in on them.

Frikkie drank some water and put the bottle down.
"Tengo, you're so *mad*, so mad at me. But what have *I*

done, man? I didn't *want* to go into the army. I had no choice—it's the law. I didn't *want* to be sent into the township. What can I do? I have to go where they tell me."

"Yes. That's right. If they tell you to go in and shoot young children, kill unarmed civilians—you're a good South African, you do as you're told."

"True as God, Tengo, d'you think I like what I'm doing! I swear to you, man, I'd much rather be at the farm, working with the animals or driving the tractor in the mielie fields. Every night before I go to sleep I think about the farm, what I'd be doing if I was there—"

"What did you think you'd have to do in the army—milk cows? You know damn well what an army is for."

"I didn't think of it, man—believe me. I knew I had to do my two years service, get it over with, then start farming with my uncle. If I thought about it at all, I thought I might have to be fighting those guerillas on the Angolan border. I didn't know we'd be sent into the townships to try and get kids to go back to school. *We're* not to blame, Tengo. Blame these agitators who come into the townships to stir up trouble."

"You believe all that rubbish," Tengo said with scorn. "They brainwash you in the army, that's what they do. *Agitators*! What you call agitators are only people who *show* us what we already know: that our education system is planned to keep us inferior, that black kids are dying of hunger, and our parents are treated like dirt. Agitators don't *make* trouble—our trouble is already there. They show us that we don't have to put up with it, that we can try to change it. It's another one of those lies the whites use—to blame *agitators* for the trouble in the townships."

Frikkie drew back from Tengo's anger, pushing himself against the sacks as if he could get further away from the onslaught of words coming at him.

"The whites don't *need* agitators, but if your mother and father lived in a hut and ate mostly mielie-meal, and your sister Sissie had T.B., would there be anything wrong in someone pointing out to you that you weren't being allowed to have a decent life? *Would there?*"

"Tengo, my uncle and aunt are good to their workers. My uncle used to drive Tandi into Doringkraal when she had to see the doctor. He *paid* for her treatment."

"Sure," Tengo said. "He wanted to make sure none of the other workers would get T.B."

"You're not fair, Tengo. Oom Koos is better than a lot of the other farmers."

"You don't understand, do you, Frikkie? Maybe white people *can't* understand. We don't want your *kindness.* You don't own us. We're not your children or your slaves. How can I make you understand? Listen, what do you think it felt like when I came into the farm kitchen one day and I saw your little sister—so much younger than I was, and she could read better than me. *How do you think that feels?*" He wanted to take Frikkie by the shoulders and shake him, not for the harm done but for not understanding. "And your mother, always sending Sissie's old dolls and clothes for Tandi—"

"Would it have been better if she hadn't sent them?" Frikkie cut in.

"It would have been better if my father was paid a man's wages for a hard day's work. Then he could have bought those things himself. What do you think it felt like when we were out in the yard playing soccer, and your aunt would call you inside to eat a nice lunch, with meat and potatoes, *cooked by my mother*—and I'd get some tea and bread and maybe a few scraps, leftovers, out at the back. Didn't you ever *think* that I would begin to wonder why you were entitled to a full stomach while your little black friend out in the yard was still feeling hungry. *Hungry!* Do you know what it's like to be hungry—day after day?" His voice rose. "Plenty of black children know."

"It's not fair, Tengo. You can't blame *me* for everything that's wrong with this country."

"I'm not blaming you for that," Tengo said, feeling suddenly weary. "I'm blaming you for not *knowing*. For not *wanting* to know."

With the weight of Tengo's words fully on him, Frikkie recoiled; he was ambushed, not only physically but by the relentlessness of the accusations. The small shed seemed to be drawing in on him. There was no escape from Tengo's wrath, which boiled up again, jolting Frikkie.

"*Didn't you ever think about it!*" Tengo shouted suddenly, the feeling of injustice that had lain still in those years flying up out of him.

"As true as God, Tengo," Frikkie said, speaking slowly, fumbling for words to reach Tengo across the chasm that lay open between them, "it was the only way I knew. I swear, I never thought it could be any different . . ."

"Well, that's hard luck for you now, isn't it! You've found out too late. Now you see it *can* be different. Here's Frikkie lying on the floor, and here's Tengo with the gun. It's all turned around, isn't it? *Isn't it!*" Now, for the first time, he had a sense of power because of the gun; he felt dizzy almost; a rush of exaltation swept through him as he recognized that Frikkie, not he, was the one needing mercy. "And Frikkie, this is just the beginning," he said softly. "What you're learning here *all* your people are going to have to learn. And they're not going to enjoy the lesson either. It's because you're all the same—*none of you want to think about it.*" As his feeling of triumph mounted, he felt a grim satisfaction at the blow he had delivered to Frikkie's head.

"Tengo, listen to me. How could I think it could be any different? Everyone—my ma, my pa, my uncle and aunt, my teachers, the dominee at our church—they all taught me that this is the way it's supposed to be. So why shouldn't I accept it then? Now you're accusing me. I never did anything wrong! *It's got nothing to do with me.*" Raising his voice made the pain in his head worse; he could hardly see out of his right eye. "Tengo," he went on, "can't you see? It all started long ago, long before you or I were born. You can't blame me just for being born white. It's got nothing to do with me." He lay back against the pile of sacks, his head throbbing. He wondered if he was going to pass out again. He closed his eyes.

Tengo was silent for a time. Then he said, "You're wrong. You *did* do wrong."

Frikkie opened his eyes. "What did I do?" he asked truculently.

"You didn't *see* that anything was wrong, that's what you did. You don't remember, but I do, when your auntie sent us out milk and cake in the yard once because we were covered in mud and she didn't want you coming into the house. You got a nice cup and plate with flowers painted on, and I got a tin mug and a tin plate. Tell me, what was I supposed to think about myself—that I got inferior treatment because I *was* inferior? I didn't *feel* I was inferior, but I began to think, well, maybe I was. . . ."

"She didn't give you *less* than she gave me," Frikkie protested. "We both got the same helping."

"You still don't see," Tengo said. Even though he had the gun in his hand he felt defeated now by his inability to blast away, to blow up, the fastness of Frikkie's incomprehension. It was like trying to shift an embedded rock. "You still don't see," he said wearily, "you don't see that the thing you did wrong was *not notice that anything was wrong.* That's a sin, even though your Boer *dominees* don't preach it in their sermons. And now that wrong has built up, and built up—and now it's so big, so *huge* that it can't be held back anymore. And now this whole country is in terrible danger because of all the wrong that people like you couldn't see."

The pain in Frikkie's head was so intense that he leaned back with his eyes shut. He moaned faintly.

"Is your head very bad, Frikkie?"

Frikkie moaned again.

Unburdened of his anger by the words he had flung at Frikkie, Tengo felt pity now as he heard him moan. The soldier had become Frikkie again, rather than an enemy Tengo was pitted against. "Would you like some more water, Frikkie?" he asked.

"No."

He was so still that Tengo wondered if he was unconscious again. *Here I've been accusing him and his relatives of accepting things the way they are,* he thought, *yet my own parents were unquestioning too. They accepted the hardship, the poverty, the unfairness. They didn't think there were other possibilities. When it troubled me, they told me not to ask such questions, to leave things as they were and just to try to do the best we could inside the limits* they accepted, *just as Frikkie's aunt and uncle accepted them. So why should Frikkie's people have to take all the blame?* He stroked the smooth hard surface of the gun stock. *Yet perhaps there* is *an excuse for my parents, for my aunts and uncles,* he thought, *since they are the victims. But even so, that is no excuse,* he argued with himself, *because as soon as someone becomes aware he is being wronged, then in some way that person is no longer a victim.* Here was something he would like to discuss with Joseph—if and when he ever got out of this horrible little shed.

"Tengo . . ."

"What?"

"D'you remember that day—it was at Oom Koos's birthday party—my cousin Annetjie, the one with red hair and freckles, she was going to get you into trouble for threatening to hit her. Well, I went and made her and the others *swear* not to tell on you. I gave Sissie my best marble to buy her off. It was purple and green, I remember." He gave a short laugh.

"What am I supposed to say now, Frikkie?" The small spurt of sympathy he had felt drained away. "Am I supposed to put my hands together and say, thank you, Kleinbaas? Thank you for doing for me what one friend does for another, so that because I'm black and you're white you can feel good about it. What you did has got to do with *friends*, not *color*. And even though I was your friend, you didn't see anything wrong with that, that *girl* calling old Ezekiel *boy*, telling him to clean up her mess—with no respect for his age, no respect for an elder of our tribe. So now you want me to say, thank you, Kleinbaas?"

Frikkie had no answer. *He's unjust,* he thought; *he won't give us any credit for the things we did that were good.*

There was silence between them now, each boy enclosed in his own version of what had been between them. Frikkie was the first to speak: "Tengo."

"What?"

"You're not fair."

"How do you mean—not fair?"

"Well, look at how it is for me. D'you remember one day—we were helping my uncle make biltong—and we spoke of the Great Trek—"

"And of your ancestors killing my ancestors—"

"Let me speak, Tengo. My ancestors trekked away from British rule into the unknown—into the wilderness. They were truly religious people. They traveled with a gun in one hand and the Bible in the other. They *believed* it was God's will that they should trek north and settle in the Promised Land."

"They could only feel that way if they saw the blacks, who had been there for hundreds of years, as not human. And that's how they've treated us since then."

"Tengo, my family have owned the farm and worked it for generations. We have a right to it. It's *ours*."

"Frikkie, that land belonged to my people long before the whites ever came to South Africa. But it's no use arguing about it. *We were here first*. You are here now. And now we are staking our claim to what is by right ours."

"Why should you have the right to take land from us that my family has worked so hard to keep up!" Frikkie mustered his strength to cry out. He lay back against the sacks, his temple throbbing.

"You took it from us," Tengo said, implacable. "And all the work was done by blacks. Now the time is here when we will have it back."

"But what about us! Where can we go? Do you want to push us into the sea! There's no other place for us—this is our home too!"

"We don't want the whites to go. We want our fair share." With the gun across his knees and Frikkie lying pleading on the floor, Tengo felt himself again filled with a surge of power. He leaned forward toward the figure on the other side of the patch of moonlight. "Your uncle—the oubaas—is getting old, Frikkie. He'll die one of these days. And you *think* you'll get the farm."

"I *know* I will," Frikkie said with anger. "He's been to the lawyer. He's signed his will. He's leaving it to me!"

Tengo was silent. Then he said, "It will never be yours." He dealt his words out as though they were bullets. "We are going to take over this country," he said slowly. "And your uncle's farm will go to those who have done all the work for a few rand and a few sacks of mielie-meal—those who've bent their backs so that your auntie can sit in her dining room with doilies on the table and drink tea out of cups with flowers painted on them. And I'll tell you something more, Frikkie. There's a better chance that your sister will be secretary to a black lawyer than that *my* sister will be a *maid* in your auntie's kitchen." The words filled him with the sweet satisfaction he'd seen reflected on the face of the oubaas as he'd watched the wild fowl he'd taken aim at and shot plummet to the earth.

Frikkie was overcome by a rise of anguish harder to bear than the pain in his head. *Oh*, he cried out in his heart, *what will become of all of us? What will become of Ma and Pa? He's going to kill me. I'll be dead, and Sissie will be working in a black man's office. Everything has gone wrong. Pieter Uys is dead. Everything is*

spoiled. Why did it have to be this way? Confusion overwhelmed him; he wanted to understand, but it was all
too baffling for him. All he had wanted was to get out of
the army alive and spend the rest of his days working on
the farm. He meant no harm to anyone. "Why do you
hate me!" he cried out now, pushing himself forward.
"I never did you any harm. We were *friends.* I've still
got that red clay bull you made. It's on the chest of
drawers in my room at the farm."

With the mention of the red clay bull, the memory
assailed Tengo of the malleability of the raw clay in his
hands, the squeeze and squelch of it as he dug it with his
fingers from the banks of the dam. He smelled the fresh
air of the veld, felt the rhythm of the cooing of the
doves in the bluegum trees coursing with his blood
through his heart. Slowly, the fervor of his enmity toward Frikkie started to dissolve like the dust washed
away in a summer rain, and he sat in silence, abashed
by his own bullying of someone he'd already hurt so
badly.

After a time he asked awkwardly, "Frikkie, has the
drought broken yet?"

Frikkie could feel his limbs, the muscles in his neck
and jaw go slack. "No. We're still waiting for rain.
Things are bad at the farm, Tengo. My uncle's had to
take a loan from the bank. He says he's ruined if the
rains don't come soon."

"What will happen to you then?"

"I'll work that farm through drought or flood."

"Frikkie?"

"Tengo?"

"Things aren't going to be the same anymore in this
country. Surely you must see that?"

"I can see it, Tengo." He gave a short laugh. "I can

see you've got the gun and I'm lying on the floor with my head cracked. *I* can see things aren't the same. My father's cousin who farms up near the Zimbabwe border, his wife and child were badly hurt when their car drove over a land mine on the road to town. I know what's coming. *But I won't give up the farm.* I'll fight for it with everything I've got."

"So will we."

Overhead the moon had shifted, taking with it the oblong of light which was reduced now to a splash of silver under the window.

"Frikkie, I don't like violence—"

"Then why were you out on the street with that violent mob? You were throwing rocks, weren't you? Someone there had a gun. A friend of mine was shot—he's probably dead. I came after you because I saw you running so fast that I thought maybe you were the one with the gun. And you tell me you don't like violence—"

"A friend of yours was shot. . . . Do you know how many blacks have been killed in the last year? *Hundreds and hundreds*! What's the matter with you, man! Can't you see that all the violence starts with the whites, with the police, with the army—"

"We have to maintain order, Tengo."

"But you never ask yourselves, *What is the reason for the disorder*? Can't you see that all the laws and regulations that keep us inferior are a form of violence?"

"It's got nothing to do with me, Tengo. It's the law. I don't ask questions. My duty is to uphold the law. I haven't got any choice."

"But you *have* got a choice. Some people refuse to do their military service. The people my auntie works for in Jo'burg, they have two sons. Both of them have left the country rather than go into an army that shoots down the black civilian population."

"The people who leave don't care about their country," Frikkie said contemptuously. "They are cowards and traitors. I will never leave."

"There are whites working on our side too, who want to share this country with the blacks."

"They are traitors too," Frikkie said.

It's no use, Tengo thought. It appeared to him now that, rather than the blacks, it was Frikkie and whites like him who were the victims, trapped and cornered as they were by the narrowness of their vision. *They understand the laws of nature when it comes to farming,* he reflected. Long ago, he recalled now, when he was a small boy feeding the chickens, the oubaas had explained to him that poultry kept caged turned vicious, attacking one another and laying brittle, pale-yolked, tasteless eggs, while those allowed to run about freely were healthy and vigorous, their eggs strong-shelled with bright tasty yolks. *Yet these Boers couldn't understand that the same laws affect human beings, that there are consequences to everything you do whether you are prepared to acknowledge them or not. Now the blacks had a hope of change and were imagining new possibilities, while these Afrikaners—they were not going to be able to survive unless they dismantled the cages they had erected around themselves.*

To avoid troubled ground, he asked now, "Frikkie, did you do your matric?"

"I just scraped through by the skin of my teeth. I was never much of a student. How about you, Tengo?"

"There's been no school for more than a year," he said, anger and frustration mounting up even as he was trying not to oppose himself to Frikkie again. "How could I write my matric!"

"I'm sorry for you, Tengo. You have to blame your own people for that—those agitators who've organized the school boycotts."

"Would *you* like to go to school with soldiers and police patrolling the playgrounds and threatening and bullying you in the classroom!"

Frikkie made no answer. His shoulder was painful now; he rubbed it; he supposed it must be from where he'd hit the floor when he was knocked out. "Your mother told me that you wanted to go to university. She said you wanted to go and study in America."

"That's what I wanted," Tengo said. "And now—" His voice trembled and his sentence hung uncompleted between them.

"My uncle always said you were a really smart—a really smart person."

"A really smart *kaffir*, you mean," Tengo said bitterly.

In the dimness of the shed Frikkie felt his face suffuse, as, for the first time, he blushed with shame at the word he had heard and used all his life. "Excuse me, Tengo," he said, in Afrikaans, wanting to apologize—to say, *forgive me*. The words would not come.

But Tengo's anger had gone. The headlights of a car making a U-turn on the road beyond the field had raked through the window of the shed, for a moment lighting up in their glare the figure of the soldier lying against the sacks. Tengo started as he saw one half of the face, hardly changed, of the friend he had played and run with over the farm and the veld; the other half distorted, blackened with bruising, the eye swollen closed, the short-cropped yellow hair darkened with drying blood. He realized that at some point in their encounter, with-

out being concretely aware of it, he had come to a decision
that he was going to have to let Frikkie go. But he had
not yet worked out how he was going to do it.

"Frikkie?"

"What, Tengo?"

"Did you ever get to see the sea?"

Frikkie shook his head. "No."

"Me neither."

Outside, all was still. There had been no more sounds of
firing or shouting or the rumble of Casspirs for some
time now. They would complete their business, Tengo
knew, at three o'clock in the morning—the hour they
always chose to batter in the doors of sleeping house-
holders, pulling people half-awake from their beds and
ransacking the privacy of drawers and cupboards for
evidence of political activity among the terrified crying
of awakened children, before dragging the suspects—
schoolgirls and schoolboys—off to jail, leaving pleading
parents and weeping brothers and sisters among the
overturned furniture and smashed household objects.

He stood up. "Frikkie. You'd better go."

"Go?"

"Yes, man!" He was in a sudden panic to be rid of him.
"Can you get up? *Get up and go.* But I swear to you, man,
if you try anything, if you send anyone back here—I
swear I'll kill before I let anyone get me."

Frikkie got himself up unsteadily, groping against the
sacks for support. Upright, he stood still, then started to
sway as if he was going to fall. Tengo moved swiftly
over and grabbed him by the shoulders, holding him
up—the gun, in his right hand, alongside Frikkie's shoulder and arm. Frikkie leaned heavily on him, his head

resting against Tengo's neck. They remained close together in the darkness, in silence, the two of them and
the gun. With Frikkie pressed faint and heavy against
him, waiting for the waves of sickness and cold clammi-
ness to subside, Tengo thought with surprise, *I'm much
taller than he is now, more than a head taller*. His old
friend felt stocky and muscular in his arms.

Frikkie straightened up. Tengo stepped back, supporting him still with his hands gripping his shoulders, the
gun like a brace bearing his weight. "Are you okay
now?"

"I think so. . . ."

"Can you find your way back?"

"I don't remember—"

"*Listen*: Turn right and go across the field; you'll see
the alley between the houses on the other side. Go down
the alley—it crosses the road—turn right again when you
come out. After a few blocks you'll be at the church." He
stepped back, letting go of Frikkie, the gun held in both
of his hands, pointed down toward the floor. "Now *go*.
Get away from me. Remember, I'm warning you—*don't
send anyone back after me*," he said slowly, "*and don't
say anything*."

"I wouldn't do that, Tengo. You know I wouldn't."

"With white people, I don't know anything. Just go."

"Tengo, your voice, the way you speak . . . you sound
as if you hate me. Do you hate me?"

Tengo turned away in the dark, looking down at the
floor to the side of the soldier. He felt emptied, hollowed,
not wanting to think or talk anymore, wanting Frikkie
away—out of the shed and out of his mind. But Frikkie
waited, making no move to leave.

"No . . ." Tengo answered at last. He felt short of

breath, needing to heave air deep into his chest. "I don't hate you, Frikkie. I hate . . ." He raised his arm with the gun in his hand, then let it fall to his side; there was no more he could say.

Frikkie hesitated for a moment. "I'm going then. Good-bye, Tengo."

Tengo turned, facing the door, waiting for the other to leave. "Good-bye, Frikkie."

The door creaked on its rusty hinges as it was pulled open. In the dimness the shadowy figure paused, then slipped out, and the door thudded shut.

Wobbling, half-walking half-running, dizzy and un-steady, Frikkie made his way over the field, skirting the rusted skeletons of abandoned cars and the mounds of rubble that loomed up in the dark. The effort to run made the pain in his head worse, and the fear filled him that he might pass out and be found by militants who would have no mercy for him. Groggy and cold, he shivered and pushed himself on, feeling safer as he slipped into the sheltering blackness of the alley. Alert for his own safety, keeping close to the walls of the houses, his mind was flooded, as though a light burned somewhere at the back of it, with the strangeness, the wonder, of his having encountered Tengo.

Tengo had let him go, but he had known all along that he would. Well . . . he had been pretty sure that he would—though there had been some bad moments. What had been before between the two of them had proved to be stronger than what was going on now between the whites and the blacks. "*Dank Die Here*—thank God," he muttered as he ran. Beneath the pain and the fear there was an elation—*not only because he let me go*, he told himself, *but because . . . because it had been* Frikkie and Tengo *again*. The old combination formed so easily behind his lips; for a while it had been *Frikkie and Tengo* again. . . .

He paused, leaning against a wall, as he waited for a stitch in his side to let go. The moon was high now in a dark sky. The township was quiet, almost deserted, the people keeping to their houses. The smell of tear gas hung still on the night air. Emerging from the alley, he walked along the road trying to appear like a soldier patrolling the area, a mounting tide of illness rising in him. Though the night was mild he felt deathly cold; his teeth were starting to chatter and he tried to force his jaw to remain rigid. The few black people out on the street walked by, avoiding looking at him.

The square in front of the church was floodlighted and patrolled by soldiers. Two of the small tanklike vehicles with their cannons protruding menacingly were parked in the center of the square; a yellow police bus lay overturned at the far corner; a group of blue-uniformed riot police stood about. Frikkie stepped into the square and sank down at the bottom of the church steps, head on knees.

He heard the voice of his sergeant bark out, "Where have you *been*! We thought you—they're out looking for you now—*stand up when I talk to you!*" Receiving no response, the sergeant knelt down and pushed Frikkie's head up. "My God! What happened to you?"

Frikkie needed all his strength to reply. "I chased after someone. . . . I thought it was the one who'd shot Private Uys. He hid. . . . He was waiting for me . . . with a piece of iron. . . ."

The sergeant stood up. "My God, look what those

kaffirs have done to him." A group had gathered around
Frikkie. "He'll need to go to the hospital. *Where's your
gun?*" he rapped out suddenly.

Frikkie kept silent, his head sunk on his knees.

"Those black devils took it from you!" the sergeant
exploded.

Feebly, Frikkie nodded.

"There will have to be an inquiry," the sergeant said
grimly. "Who took it? Where were you? Did you see
who it was? What did he look like? Could you identify
him if we brought him in?"

Frikkie raised his head. "I couldn't see. It was in the
dark. I was knocked out. When I came round, I was
lying there, and my gun was gone."

"Those bastards—they'll pay for this," the sergeant
said. "Here—you two, put him in one of the jeeps and
get him to the hospital."

He lay on the back seat of the jeep, every pothole they
rode over, the rocks and rubble flung by the protestors
and strewn on the road surface, all registering in his
skull as thrusts of pain. The two soldiers from his unit
sat silent and upright on the jump seats.

Once outside the township the road was tarmacked
and the jeep rode smoothly. Frikkie felt his mind crackling as if it was charged with bursts of electricity that
faded out from time to time. Tengo's words rose up: *It
will never be yours . . . the farm will go to those who've
done all the work . . .* and a chill band closed around his
heart. In the dark of the unknown he saw his dream of
Oom Koos's farm wavering, like the reflections that had
dissolved into widening rings when he and Tengo had
dropped stones in the river—the idea that he had carried

with him as long as he could remember—owning and working the farm—trembling in uncertainty, disappearing in dissolving, insubstantial, widening ripples. He dozed or passed out for a while, and saw himself working as a boss-boy for Tengo, Tengo dressed in Oom Koos's khaki clothes standing on the stoep at the farm giving him orders, and he cried out aloud, rousing himself into wakefulness.

One of the soldiers leaned over and asked, "Are you okay?"

"My head hurts." Then he asked, "What's happened to Pieter Uys?"

"Never mind now," the soldier said. "Don't worry—just try to keep still. We'll soon be there."

"They killed him," Frikkie said.

The soldier kept silent.

Oh, Frikkie mourned in silence, *what is this all about . . . what is it for . . . why couldn't things just go on the way they've always been?* He saw the yellow of the mine dumps rear up past the window. The pain in his head was terrible; and Tengo had done this to him. Though they had covered him with a blanket he was shivering uncontrollably. He saw Tengo showing him how to milk the cow, the two of them falling about laughing as the warm milk squirted over their faces and hands; he lifted his hand to wipe the warm milk away but tasted salt—salt smarting his grazed knuckles—and he realized that it was tears running like warm milk over his face and hands. The noise of the jeep drowned out the sound of the sobs that were tearing his chest as the tears ran down his cheeks and hands. The soldier touched him and said, *"Stil, man, bly stil.* We're nearly there."

The jeep stopped at a traffic light. He heard the other

soldier say in a low voice, "*Arme ding*—poor fellow—
Pieter Uys was his best friend."

His best friend . . . He had wanted to say thank you to
Tengo, had paused with his hand on the door of the shed
to say it, but Tengo at that moment had seemed so re-
mote and so formidable, that he had tugged the door
open and left without another word. He and Tengo,
they were separated—separated by something that
neither of them was responsible for—and now they
were the ones who had to pay.

As the jeep sped through the outskirts of the town into
the brightly lit streets of the city center, Frikkie gave
himself up to his grief. He wept without restraint. "I
wish . . . I wish . . ." he kept saying over and over in
Afrikaans.

"What is it, old man?" one of the soldiers asked.
"*Wat wens jy?*—what do you wish?"

Choked by the tears filling his throat, he could not tell
them that he was wishing that it could all have been
different . . . and yet could have stayed just the way
it was.

Alone in the shed, Tengo found he was trembling
violently. He had not looked up; the door had opened,
then closed, and Frikkie was gone. He sat down on the
kerosene tin. He was shocked at what he had done to
Frikkie. He thought of his mother and the wife of the
oubaas in the kitchen at the farm, making jam together.
If they could see what he had done to Frikkie—all the
dark dried blood matting the yellow hair . . . he looked
terrible. He wondered if Frikkie would make it back to
the church square. What if he collapsed on the way and

was picked up by some of the comrades . . . Fear chilled him. He should never have let him go—but what else could he have done? What if Frikkie was picked up by the comrades and given the "necklace"? But the township was filled with soldiers and police tonight, he reassured himself; the militants would all be lying low.

So I'm taller than Frikkie now, he thought . . . *me and Frikkie again . . . after all this time. And Frikkie still has that clay bull I made.* . . . Sitting in the dark on the kerosene tin, he recalled how happy he had been while he made that small clay animal—not so much happy, he thought, as deeply absorbed in what he was doing. But that day when the first box of books had come, as he had walked back to the kraal with his father so tall and thin and balancing the heavy box so easily on his head, *that* day he was truly happy. His heart had felt as light as a helium balloon. Now he could feel his heart as a heavy weight pushing down, down in his chest, pushing down so heavily that it hurt.

It had all gone wrong. *The grown-ups—whites and blacks—they had let it all go wrong,* he thought as he sat grieving in the desolation of the shed. *And now—the children—it is up to us—and it is very hard.* . . .

Joseph had said that they've *got a lot to lose, and for us there can only be gain,* he reflected; *but it's a terrible price we have to pay for what we'll gain.* He wished it could have been different. . . .

So I'm taller than Frikkie, he marveled again. He realized now that as he had stood supporting his friend in his arms, with the gun in his hand, with Frikkie almost passing out and his bruised, bloodied head resting on his shoulder, it had come to him clearly what it was that he now had to do. Violence was not for him. He could see its necessity for the struggle that was taking place, that was making normal life impossible. But if he was offered the choice . . .

He was going to go with Joseph to Lusaka, cross over the border with him; and when he got there, and they asked him, Do you want to continue your education, or do you want to train as a freedom fighter?—he knew now, without any doubt, what he would tell them. In that brief moment he had made his choice.

He could tell no one—not Joseph nor Elijah—what had happened in the shed. He gazed dully now at the gun in his hands. The gun—what was he going to do with it? He looked around the shed, got up and walked about, knocking the floorboards with the butt. Near the pile of sacks there was a splintering sound as he brought the butt down. He dropped to his knees. The floorboards there were rotting. With the crowbar he prised a few boards loose, slipped the gun into the space underneath, stamped the boards back down and moved a few of the sacks over to cover the place. Some small animal scuttled out to hide elsewhere in the dark.

Joseph would consider it an act against the struggle not to hand the gun over to the comrades; getting hold of firearms was one of their biggest problems. He would have liked to let the gun lie there, and rust, and rot. *But I don't have the right to do that,* he thought. He would leave the gun where it was for now. Later, Joseph would know how to deal with it. *Would Joseph have considered it wrong as well to have let Frikkie go free,* he wondered. He placed another of the sacks over the disturbed floorboards.

By now Frikkie must be back with the others. He wondered how seriously he had been hurt. Frikkie wouldn't have given him away. He had promised. . . . For a moment then, doubt and fear assailed him. *Frikkie's a soldier*, he reminded himself. *He's one of them*. But in the same instant, almost, the white soldier became Frikkie again, and he knew that Frikkie would keep his word.

He peered now through the grimy window and saw there was no one about. On the road beyond the field he could see the lights of a line of army vehicles moving slowly out of the township.

He opened the door of the shed and stepped into the night. Walking swiftly, he made his way back to his aunt's house.